REVENGE IS THE SPUR

The eight looters left the tiny settlement burning, left two Texas Trouble-Shooters to die a fiery death in the town jail. This would have ended the legend of the notorious outlaw-fighters, but for the intervention of scar-faced Belle Fassen. Riding free again and craving vengeance, the Texans hunted their treacherous quarry and caught up with the last guilty men in San Francisco, eight hundred and fifty miles from where it all began.

MARSHALL GROVER

◆

REVENGE IS THE SPUR

A Larry & Stretch Western

Complete and Unabridged

LINFORD
Leicester

First published in Australia by
Horwitz Grahame Pty Limited
Australia

First Linford Edition
published 1998
by arrangement with
Horwitz Publications Pty Limited
Australia

British Library CIP Data

Grover, Marshall
    Larry & Stretch: revenge is the spur.
    —Large print ed.—
Linford western library
1. Western stories
2. Large type books
I. Title
823 [F]

ISBN 0–7089–5316–6

Published by
F. A. Thorpe (Publishing) Ltd.
Anstey, Leicestershire

Set by Words & Graphics Ltd.
Anstey, Leicestershire
Printed and bound in Great Britain by
T. J. International Ltd., Padstow, Cornwall

This book is printed on acid-free paper

1

Raw Deal

THE taller Texan yawned, squinted against the sun-haze and observed,

'It don't look like much of a town, runt.'

'And to think that cow-waddy told us it's the county seat,' remarked his equally unimpressed companero.

'There'll be saloons.' Stretch Emerson, so nicknamed by his partner of near twenty years for his gangling six and a half feet frame, said this with deep gratitude. 'That's what matters. I got a thirst that won't quit.'

'You and me both,' declared Larry Valentine.

Only his whimsical sidekick had ever called him 'runt'. He was in fact only three inches shorter than Stretch, an uncommonly brawny son of the Lone Star State, dark-haired, handsome in a battered way, straddling a sorrel near as weary as its master. Like Stretch, who rode a pinto, he was rigged in the range riders' garb favored by men raised in the Texas Panhandle; they were invariably assumed to be out of work cowhands. As for his armory, it differed from his partner's in only one respect. Sheathed Winchesters were slung to their mounts along with their saddlebags and packrolls, but Stretch, being ambidextrous with handguns, packed twice as much Colt .45.

To reach the little township of Curran, located just a few miles north of the Mexican border, these nomads had travelled a lot of hot and dusty South New Mexico. They weren't short on food and their canteens were still a quarter full, but their joint liquor supply and Bull Durham had been used up four days ago, hence their need to find civilization.

Entering Curran's main street — what

there was of it — they at once noted a saloon, just one, Hanslow's Bar. It seemed Curran had only one of everything, one general store, one livery stable, one forge, one bank, one hotel. The one church located on a rise west of town beside the cemetery and the tiny schoolhouse was probably used by worshippers of all persuasions, always supposing there were any religious-minded folk in this community. The buildings lining the street were part adobe, part frame, typical of this part of the New Mexico Territory. There were homes on streets angling off the main thoroughfare, and that was it, all there was to see of the seat of Curran County.

Jake Toone, proprietor of the livery stable, was polite, but in a reserved way. He took charge of their horses and indicated they were welcome to leave their gear here while the animals were allowed to cool before feeding, watering and rubbing down.

From the stable, they trudged along the splintered plank sidewalk to the batwings of the saloon. Entering, they decided they had seen cheerier barrooms. The local loungers were an unprepossessing bunch as was Hanslow himself, the beefy, sharp-eyed man presiding at the dealwood bar. The only respectable-looking local present was the elderly, spare of build townman nursing a tot of rum and seated alone at a table by the side wall. In a corner, a slovenly Mexican strummed a guitar, providing accompaniment for the woman standing beside him, singing to the customers.

She might have been beautiful once. Her disfigurement, Larry guessed, was no accident of birth; the scar was jagged and marred most of her right cheek. As he glanced at her, he made a point of doffing his sweat-stained Stetson; so did Stretch. Then they moved to the bar counter and ordered whiskey.

'Comin' up,' leered Hanslow. 'Best booze in town. Cost you a quarter a shot.'

4

He filled two shot glasses from a stone jug, while the Texans surveyed him in puzzlement, only puzzled right now, not yet indignant. Larry paid while remarking, 'Whiskey comes plenty expensive in this little burg.'

'Take it or leave it,' shrugged Hanslow.

Stretch stifled a yawn, wearily propped an elbow and said,

'We'll take it, but only because we're so all-fired thirsty.'

The elderly rum-drinker spoke up.

'You ought to hang your head in shame, Bart Hanslow,' he bitterly chided. 'If I can run my business charging fair prices on all my stock, so can you.'

'I swear, Dryden, you were born complainin',' jibed Hanslow.

The scarred woman finished her song and started for the stairs.

'I want to check on Dorrie,' she told Hanslow.

'That lazy bitch,' he sneered.

'She's sick — could be dying,' she retorted.

'That's what Doc says, and what would *he* know?' challenged Hanslow. 'A useless whiskeyhead like him?'

The woman hurried upstairs. The Texans sampled their whiskey, traded scowls and used the nearest spittoon.

'Call this whiskey?' growled Larry.

'Or is this supposed to be a joke?' asked Stretch.

'At least the rum's branded,' said old Dryden.

Larry set his glass on the bar.

'This is moonshine booze — rotgut,' he muttered. Then he pointed. 'We'll take our shots from that bottle. It's got a label, so it has to be safer for a man's innards.'

Hanslow glanced to the back shelf and shook his head.

'Nothin' doin'. Last bottle in stock and reserved for the sheriff. If you ain't partial to the good corn liquor I cook in my still, try another saloon — if you can find one.'

'If the local doc drinks this poison, his brains must be scrambled,' Stretch remarked to Larry. 'I sure hope we don't need him while we're here.'

'I guess the sheriff ain't as brave as the doc,' muttered Larry. 'After a few weeks of drinkin' this stuff, he'd likely go loco and blow his brains out.'

'You saddlebums're givin' me a pain in my ass with your bellyachin',' taunted Hanslow.

'Moonshiner, that better be the last time you call us saddlebums,' Larry coldly warned.

'Well, ain't this a shame — I've hurt their feelin's!' Hanslow grinned at local layabouts who grinned right back at him. 'You boys as sick of their whinin' as I am, feel like a little fun? Let's throw 'em out.'

Four unkempt plug-uglies stood up. Larry glanced at them, narrowed his eyes and said softly, 'Better think twice. It mightn't go the way you expect.'

Hanslow came around from behind his bar. The scarred woman was descending the stairs, her hazel eyes watchful, and old Dryden raising

7

his voice in protest.

'If Ackers was a *real* sheriff, this rough treatment of trail-weary strangers wouldn't be tolerated!'

'Just shuddup, Dryden, and don't get in our way,' chuckled Hanslow. He squared off at Larry while his hangers-on converged, bunching their fists. Then the scarred woman irritated him. 'And don't *you* get in our way, Belle!'

There were a few moments of confusion as the woman called Belle got between the Texans and their would-be assailants, and moved around behind Larry. Then she was retreating to a corner and Hanslow aiming a low blow at Larry.

Even when close to exhaustion, the drifters probably unknown to the Curran citizenry could not be derided, prodded or beaten up by the likes of Bart Hanslow and his cronies. Tired? Certainly they were, bone-tired, badly in need of rest, but still the Texas Trouble-Shooters,

8

still the outlaw-fighting tumbleweeds of formidable reputation, still instinctive warriors who, when under threat, could summon reserves of muscle-power. Hanslow's low blow never landed. Larry's left jab bloodied his nose and drove him back against the bar, cursing obscenely. His cronies came on at a rush and, in a matter of moments, suffered more punishment than they inflicted.

The one who threw a punch to Stretch's face struck him only once. Stretch's retaliation was fast and decisive, three slamming belly blows that put him down bug-eyed and wheezing in anguish. Simultaneously, Larry stopped a roundhouse right that started his head throbbing, but didn't budge him; he swung a mighty uppercut that threw his attacker clear across the bar-room to sprawl unconscious atop a table.

Their blood up, the tall men made every punch count. When Hanslow grabbed Larry from behind, pinning his arms, another rowdy swung a blow to his mid-section. Larry made a growling sound and used his right foot to break Hanslow's grasp and start him howling; his spur had raked Hanslow's shin. The man who had struck Larry was then seized bodily, lifted and hurled. Yelling, he hurtled back-first onto a table; it collapsed under his weight. Whirling, Larry gave himself the satisfaction of blacking Hanslow's left eye. He followed that with an upper-cut that flipped the dispenser of rotgut over his own bar.

An adversary bested by the taller Texan was sent reeling into the street and, suddenly, others of Hanslow's friends lost interest in pitting their strength against the strangers.

'For once — exactly what you deserve!' fumed Dryden.

The Texans were mopping their faces and redonning their headgear when the local law came barging in, both aiming cocked shot-guns. Warily, the victors of that brief brawl kept their hands clear of their holsters. Their courage had never been questioned. Even so, they weren't foolhardy; no man bucking cocked shot-guns at short range could hope to survive.

'Careful with them cannons,' growled Stretch.

'Get your paws up, tall boy,' ordered the pudgy, unshaven sheriff.

'Both of you!' leered his scrawny deputy, dilating his eyes.

'Lock 'em up, Billy!' panted Hanslow, rising from below the bar counter. 'They were hell-bent for a fight the minute they walked in! Look what they did to me and my friends! Look at the damage!'

'This is a damn outrage!' gasped Dryden. 'You started it, you and your layabout buddies!'

Sheriff Billy Ackers and Deputy Sam Phipps ignored Dryden and rammed the muzzles of their shot-guns against the Texans' bellies. In this situation, neither trouble-shooter could resist Hanslow's disarming them. They were then hustled from the saloon, Phipps

11

with their belted Colts hung over a shoulder, his and Ackers's weapons prodding their backs all the way along to the shabbiest law office they had seen in many a long year.

Phipps hung their sidearms on the gunrack and, while Ackers went through their pockets, kept them covered. Larry's watch, their jack-knives and Stretch's harmonica were tossed into the office safe; Ackers pocketed their small change and complained sourly, 'Nickels and dimes. They're trail-trash sure enough.'

Larry was tight-lipped, reining in his temper. Ackers hadn't emptied his hip pocket, so it was all too obvious somebody at Hanslow's had relieved him of the wallet containing his and his partner's bankroll during the fracas. Here in Curran, their Lone Star luck had been all bad. These lawmen, if such they deserved to be called, had to be cohorts of Hanslow and of similar low character. The hoosegow would be no more hygienic than this musty office and, undoubtedly, the food would be lousy.

'Penalty for disturbin' the peace of Curran is thirty days jail,' Phipps declared after the tall men were locked into a double cell. 'You ain't gonna like it, I promise you.'

'We believe you,' Larry coldly assured him.

Left to themselves, only inmates of this evil-smelling calaboose, the veterans squatted on bunks and traded grim stares.

'Right fine little town.' Usually guileless and easy-going, Stretch was at this moment as cynical as his companero of better than two decades. 'Real nice folks.'

'Hombre at the stable seemed regular enough,' muttered Larry. 'Scarfaced Belle must have some heart in her. She was frettin' about a sick friend upstairs. The old feller they call Dryden took our side. That makes three I'd call human. But Hanslow and his buddies and these no-good

13

badge-toters? Lowdown, all of 'em.'

They watched cockroaches skitter across the cell-floor and grimaced in disgust. Rising, they removed blankets from their bunks and shook them. More bugs.

'Thirty days in this stinkin' hole,' grouched Stretch.

'That ain't the worst of it,' said Larry. ''Cept for what's hid in our boots, we're . . . '

'I'd calculate thirty-five dollars 'tween us,' interjected Stretch.

''Cept for that, we're busted,' scowled Larry. 'Some sonofabitch lifted my wallet.'

'Ain't that just beautiful,' mumbled Stretch. 'How good was our bankroll anyway?'

'Seven hundred and fifty or thereabouts,' said Larry.

'We got just one thing to be thankful for,' sighed Stretch.

'I ain't feelin' real thankful right now,' growled Larry. 'So tell me. Warm my heart.'

'We scarce tasted Hanslow's rotgut,' Stretch reminded him. 'With a couple gulps of it in our bellies, we'd be feelin' a helluva lot worse'n we do.'

'Ain't that the truth,' agreed Larry.

It would not be their first hitch in a small-town jail. History was repeating itself. Having wandered just about every corner of the frontier beyond their homestate, they had clashed with hostile law officers as frequently as they had clashed with stage and bank robbers, homicidal gunslingers and two-legged predators of every kind. Rustlers, cardsharps, claim-jumpers and bunko artists, they had met them all, invariably with violent consequences. This seemed to be their destiny, all they could expect of life, despite their oft-voiced desire to just mind their own business, drift at will and find peace. Inevitably, they had been on the receiving end of a great deal of publicity. Frontier newsmen did tend to exaggerate their exploits; reports of yet another victory against the lawless by the Lone Star

Trouble-Shooters circulated widely, were good for business. Unfortunately, many of those reports had featured photographs of the notorious outlaw-fighters, so they were famous, but who needed fame? Their reputation was a millstone round their necks; conceit was not one of their failings.

'Didn't even ask our names, Ackers and his deputy,' Stretch recalled.

'Fine by me,' shrugged Larry. 'If nobody in this two-bit town knows who we are, fine by me.'

The meal served them at sundown confirmed their worst expectations. Swill. And signs of movement indicated it was inhabited swill. The coffee was no better. Looking in on them later to collect the dishes, Phipps observed jeeringly, 'Well, looky here. You ain't ate nothin'. Too bad. You're gonna lose so much weight 'fore we turn you loose, you'll be chicken-weak. Next jaspers you tangle with, they'll beat hell outa you.'

'But, soon enough, we'll be free of

this bug-trap,' said Larry, cold-eyeing him. 'That's no threat, Phipps. Just somethin' for you to think about.'

An hour later, the taller Texan's belly was growling and he was gloomily predicting, 'By the time we get out of here, we *will* be chicken-weak.'

'Or sick,' Larry said bitterly. 'If we get so hungry as to eat what they feed us.'

Stretch stood on his bunk to try his strength on the bars of the cell window. Then he lay prone, scanning all he could see of the jailhouse, adobe walls, iron bars, a timber roof.

'We've been in some rough spots, runt,' he said uneasily. 'But this'un's a doozy.'

'We'll make out,' said Larry. 'Just by stayin' mad and rememberin' we can't blame ourselves, we'll make out.'

'They had shot-guns on us,' scowled Stretch. 'Double-barrelled — and cocked.'

The jailhouse was lit by only one lamp hanging above the passage, its wick turned low. They were sharing a disgruntled silence when, about fifteen minutes later, something was shoved between the window bars and fell on Stretch's chest. He grabbed at it while Larry cocked an ear to the sound of furtively receding footsteps. Stretch sniffed at the cloth-wrapped bundle and gleefully announced, 'It's chow!'

'Don't holler,' cautioned Larry. 'Don't let them star-totin' skunks know. Let's keep this 'tween us and whoever decided we oughtn't starve. Unwrap the stuff. I'll keep my eye on that end door.'

The bundle contained four sandwiches, corn-bread and thickly sliced. The filling was welcome, slabs of ham and cheese, rings of tomato and onion and dill pickle. They accounted for this donated repast. Larry folded the square of calico and stowed it inside his shirt. They agreed that, if their anonymous benefactor kept this up, they would not leave this jail in a condition of advanced malnutrition.

'Good coffee'd go down fine now,' muttered Stretch, flicking a crumb from his sleeve.

'So would roast turkey or a couple heapin' bowls of beef stew,' retorted Larry. 'But that kind of chow can't be squeezed 'tween them bars. Whoever thinks we're worth helpin' just has to do the best he knows how.'

'Mightn't be as easy in daylight,' fretted Stretch.

'I reckon not,' said Larry. 'Anybody in that side alley'd be spotted for sure.'

Woodville 'Stretch' Emerson of the uncomplicated psyche had never been the type to examine the dental equipment of a gift horse. Even so, he was moved to wistfully confide, 'I could sure use a smoke.'

'You and me both.' Larry was just as wistful. 'They could throw in a couple sacks of Bull Durham and matches, but they won't. Not much air in this stink-hole. Phipps or Ackers'd catch a whiff of tobacco and know we're gettin'

19

help from outside.'

'You suppose he's helped other jailbirds?' asked Stretch.

'Maybe,' nodded Larry. 'The way old Dryden talked, it's happened to other strangers unlucky enough to drift into Curran.'

'What keeps this place alive?' wondered Stretch.

'The ranch-hand that pointed us thisaway, he said there's five spreads in this county,' Larry reminded him.

'Come payday, the local cowhands *couldn't* be drinkin' Hanslow's rotgut, must all be temperance,' reasoned Stretch. 'Else every bunkhouse'd be full of sick hombres. There'd be no hands to tend the herds.'

'I can't believe a polecat like Hanslow could ever be popular,' said Larry. 'And that goes double for Ackers and Phipps.'

In the kitchen behind the Dryden Emporium, the storekeeper and his wife were finishing supper. Zachary Dryden had recounted the incident at the saloon. Motherly Carrie shared her husband's disgust. They had only one child, a daughter, full-grown now, married and living in Phoenix, Arizona with her husband; Marcus Parry ran the Western Union office there. A nephew of whom they were very fond had stayed with them for almost two years after their daughter's departure. He too had left to try his luck elsewhere less than three months ago.

'I'm grateful our Harriet's married and settled a long way from Curran,' Carrie said emphatically. 'I miss her, but at least we know she's got a good man and can call herself a citizen of a real community.'

'Just how I feel about my nephew,' declared Dryden. 'Fine young feller, Todd.'

'Todd's thirty-two,' she retorted with a sad smile. 'Well, Zack dear, at your age I suppose any man under forty seems like a youngster.

'Todd with his good education and his fine manners, nothing for him in a town like Curran,' mused Dryden, lighting his pipe. 'But it was a joy, wasn't it, our orphan nephew staying with us near two years, helping out in the store, relieving me of some heavy chores?'

'It was wonderful,' Carrie readily agreed. 'That was such a happy time for us. I guess we were getting lonely. And he was always so obliging, so cheerful — brightened up the old place.'

'Couldn't hope for him to stay much longer,' shrugged Dryden. 'No opportunities for a young feller with ambition. Mind now, Curran won't stay the way it is right now. This town has a real future.'

'You've been saying that for the longest time.'

'But it's true, Carrie. It has to happen. Curran's a county seat after all, so it's bound to grow and things have to get better for everybody.'

'There's a discouraging influence here, Zack. All the law we have is one sheriff and a deputy, and neither of them any better than Barton Hanslow. Just miserable trash is all they are.'

'I have faith, my dear. Still plenty of good people here. You know how I feel about banks, but I respect Karl Sperlman like I respect Caleb Bassault. Matter of fact, Caleb's the one I'm counting on. Half Circle's growing all the time, biggest ranch in the county and Caleb's becoming a man of influence. It's my belief . . . '

'You mean your big hope.'

'All right, my big hope. Inside another year, Caleb and the other cattlemen will decide Ackers and Phipps aren't fit men for keeping the peace here. There'll be some changes made, Carrie, mark my words.'

'I hope you're right, Zack,' sighed Carrie. 'Oh, *how* I hope you're right.'

The storekeeper puffed on his blackened brier and brooded a moment.

'I don't resent growing old — you know that,' he muttered. 'It's The Lord's will no man can stay young and I accept His will. Only time it irks me to be old and weak is when I see strangers roughed up by Hanslow and his no-account buddies. By golly, if Todd had been there, those tall bucks wouldn't have had to fight off those layabouts with no help. He'd have gotten into it, lent his weight to theirs.'

'You said they didn't need help anyway,' she reminded him.

'Wasn't a sight for a lady's eyes,' he grinned. 'But just this once I wish you'd been witness to what those Texas boys did, the way they defended themselves. They stopped a punch or two, sure, but you should've seen how they dealt with those roughnecks. They were all down and bleeding when Ackers and Phipps arrived.' His grin changed to a grimace. 'They did what I'd expect of them. Would they behave as true lawmen, do what's fair? Not those two. So now those tall fellers are stuck in the county jail, that pest hole.'

His wife changed the subject at this point.

'If there's to be progress here, I hope the first improvements will be a stagecoach depot and a telegraph office,' she said earnestly. 'That way, Harriet's letters would reach us faster. It's a long wait between deliveries from the Benson freight company.'

'We'll read that last letter of hers tonight,' he suggested.

'That'll be nice,' she nodded. 'But I know it by heart.'

The next two days passed slowly for the Curran jail's only inmates. Only when Nature called did they see the rear yard, and never together. Each morning, they were escorted to the ablution block and the privy, but separately, washing, shaving and relieving themselves with a cocked shotgun constantly trained on them.

They did manage to keep up their strength. There was little of the fare fed them by their captors they dared eat, but somebody still cared. Their second night of durance vile, the bundle forced through their cell window contained a cold chicken of respectable size and four slabs of bread. The third night, sandwiches again, but of roast beef, thick slabs of it, and a half-dozen hard-boiled eggs.

The morning after that nourishing meal, sprawled on their bunks, they were distracted by sounds that suggested all hell was about to bust loose in Curran. It began with a local yelling excitedly, 'Soldiers comin'!'

Came then a drumming of hooves and a shouted warning muffled by a clamor of questions.

'What the hell's happenin' out there?' wondered Stretch.

'If everybody's got to holler, I wish they'd holler *clear*,' frowned Larry.

It was exactly 10.10 a.m. when the seven uniformed riders charged their mounts into Curran from the south, six troopers led by a handsome blond man wearing the insignia of a second lieutenant. An eighth trooper was sighted atop the shallow rise fifty feet from the south end of Main, sitting his mount, surveying the terrain farther south through binoculars.

Zack Dryden, Hanslow, the two lawmen and the portly Karl Sperlman, founder and manager of the town's only bank, were well to the fore of the group turning out to listen in shock to the officer's warning. He identified himself as Lieutenant Martin Nolan, in charge of a patrol from the Second Cavalry Regiment's camp outside Selburn, a sizeable town some distance to the north-east. It was imperative, he announced, that this settlement be evacuated immediately.

'Your only chance of survival, ladies and gentlemen,' he warned. 'And I estimate you have less than an hour to flee while you can — considerably less than an hour — so there's no time to be wasted.'

'I thought the army had overcome the Indian problem,' protested the banker.

'This could be worse for Curran,' declared the officer. 'You are under threat from Armendariz and his band

27

of renegades, who have butchered and pillaged all along the border country these past five months. They number sixty and most of them are part-Apache. They are heavily armed, well-mounted and lusting for blood. Be grateful, sir, one of my men sighted them when they crossed the border — headed *this way*.'

'Heaven help us all!' gasped a woman.

'Is there shelter somewhere north?' demanded Nolan, rising in his stirrups to stare in that direction. 'Some position you civilians could defend?'

'Safest place'd be Guillermo Canyon,' said jittery Seth Rowley, proprietor of Curran's only hotel. 'It's a box. We could barricade the only way in.'

'That's what you must do — and quickly,' urged Nolan.

'You and your men will come with us?' asked Dryden.

'We will stay to defend your town as best we can,' Nolan told him. 'My orders are explicit. Any American town in which a Second Cavalry patrol finds itself, regardless of its size, must be defended by that patrol.'

'But you're outnumbered!' frowned Sperlman.

'Civilians have no option but to flee from such murderous scum, sir,' said Nolan. 'Soldiers have no option but to make a stand. We'll make ours here, manning rooftops. When the raiders arrive, we'll give a good account of ourselves, you may be sure. It won't be the first time a heavy force of raggletale bandits have been repulsed by a handful of resolute cavalrymen. That's what we're trained for and, by Henry, we'll do our duty.'

'The hell of it is all the cattle spreads're a far piece from town,' a townman complained. 'But this much I can do, Lieutenant. I'll ride out and sound the alarm and maybe a couple dozen cattlemen get here in time to help with the fightin'.'

That man dashed away to saddle a horse. Nolan seemed unconcerned that no locals volunteered to stay on to support the soldiers; he was snapping orders to the troopers, directing them to firing positions and urging the citizens to move fast.

Sperlman, a man of influence in Curran, also barked orders. A wagon was brought to the bank and the safe toted out and loaded aboard by four hefty townmen; the life savings of his depositors would not be abandoned to any bandit-boss. The exodus was beginning, and no local moved faster than Ackers and Phipps. Thoroughly intimidated, they saddled up and started northward, Ackers yelling over his shoulder, 'C'mon, folks! Up to me to get you outa town and lead you to the canyon!'

Neither lawman spared a thought for their prisoners; they hadn't even paused by Ackers's office to empty the gunrack. Nor did neighbors of the Drydens help hitch their bays to their jumpseat rig and load stock being toted out by the aged storekeeper. Carrie crammed some of their clothing into an old valise and, as she stowed it behind the seat, began a question.

'Zack, shouldn't you . . . ?'

'I daren't take the time,' he muttered, handing her up to the seat. 'Besides, it'll all be safe where it is. Takes me longer nowadays to get to it. Those slabs're getting heavier for me, honey. And it's our secret hiding place after all. No bandit'd think of looking there. We have to hurry now.'

In rigs of every kind, on horseback and afoot, Curran's small population moved out, heading north. The schoolhouse had emptied in double-quick time, Miss Lauter the schoolteacher helping lift children into moving vehicles. Well in the lead were the sheriff and his deputy, raking their mounts with their spurs. It was a speedy exit.

Until the townfolk were out of sight, the handsome man on the prancing black stared after them. Then, when there was nought but dust to be seen on the northern horizon, he signalled the horseman on the rise to the south. That one rode in, cheerfully remarking, 'It worked.'

'Good planning, Anson, you sly fox,' grinned the man called Nolan. 'So now we can get on with it?'

'Now's the time, Hal,' nodded the other man.

Again, Stretch lowered himself from the cell window to flop beside his partner, who demanded,

'What d'you make of it?'

'Near as I can figure, a bandido gang's about to raid this place,' frowned Stretch. 'Every mother's son's vamoosed. Town's empty 'cept for a few troopers aimin' to set up defenses.'

'And nobody remembered about us,' scowled Larry.

'Specially them spooked badge-toters,' Stretch said scathingly.

'Let me at that window,' said Larry, rising. 'We better let the army know we're here.'

2

Ordeal By Fire

LARRY'S booming baritone should have won attention immediately. He bellowed at the full strength of his lungs, but it seemed almost five minutes before he heard a man enter the side alley.

'Find the keys and turn us loose!' he urged the man he couldn't see. 'You're gonna need all the help you can get!'

His scalp crawled. The man outside was laughing. He was to remember that laugh. Derisive, an inane gurgling sound to it. Then the man stopped laughing and called a reply.

'Forget it, jailbird.'

'Forget it — hell!' protested Stretch.

'Stay put,' the man jeered. 'Stay and fry.'

Larry yelled another demand but heard only receding footsteps.

'Runt . . . ' Stretch was wincing uneasily. 'Somethin' ain't right.'

'I got the same feelin',' muttered Larry.

The next sounds they heard confused them further. Harsh, triumphant laughter, a whoop or two.

'Them soldier-boys don't seem like they're afeared of anything,' said Stretch. 'Hard to believe a bunch of bandidos're headed thisaway.'

'*Too* hard to believe,' said Larry.

'Got any ideas?' asked Stretch.

'Nary a notion,' fretted Larry. 'I'm as mixed up as you.'

More whoops, more laughter, then the thudding sounds on the jailhouse roof and on other roofs. A few more minutes and the hoofbeats assailed their ears, riders hustling their animals eastward out of Curran. After that, silence broken only by the ugly crackling sounds, faint at first, but ominous.

They donned their hats and traded

grim glances. Stretch sniffed apprehensively and moved to their celldoor to stare toward the office.

'You smell what I smell?'

'Smoke,' Larry said with sweat beading on his brow. 'Them thuds we heard — firebrands.'

Carried by the wind, smoke wafted into the jailhouse through windows. They raised their eyes. More smoke up there — and flashes of flame. The roof was burning. Stretch swore in bitter indignation.

'Real soldiers wouldn't do what them bastards've done!' he raged.

'And what they've done's plain enough,' breathed Larry. 'Sounds like the whole damn town's on fire.'

'Damn it, runt, if there's nobody else in town, we're gonna fry — just like that laughin' sonofabitch said!' gasped Stretch.

'Ain't that the truth.' Larry knuckled at his eyes. 'So there better be somebody left — and we *better* hope they can hear us.'

The taller Texan mopped at his face and raised his eyes to the ceiling. Planks burned furiously; the heat was becoming intense. He stubbornly resisted panic, quietly warning his partner, 'It could be that time for us, runt.'

'Could be, sure,' nodded Larry. 'We could damn soon be a couple ugly burned-alive stiffs — but are we gonna quit tryin'? If there's somebody out there, we got to make 'em hear us.'

They piled one bunk on the other, climbed atop them and, faces pressed to the window bars, began yelling. The jailhouse was becoming smokier. A blazing roof plank came hurtling down to clatter into their cell. While Stretch stamped on it, Larry heard a muffled explosion — the still back of Hanslow's Bar; what else?

Their clothes clung to them, saturated with sweat. They coughed with their eyes streaming and their pulses racing and, in the few harrowing moments thereafter, resigned themselves to their fate. Theirs had been a long, hectic and nerve-wracking career, a hard life fraught with danger, tension and always the threat of sudden and violent death. Still they had survived. But now?

'No chance, runt,' wheezed Stretch. 'Listen — uh — while there's time — I want to say you've been a good amigo.'

'I guess this is it, beanpole,' mumbled Larry. 'So let's agree on somethin', huh? If we got to go, we won't go whinin'.'

'Right . . . ' Stretch nodded wearily. 'No whinin'.'

What they next heard and saw, dimly through the writhing smoke, started their scalps crawling. The inner door of the sheriff's office had burst open. A figure, a blurred shape, came hurtling into the passage between the cells, human — and female. It had to be female. They glimpsed the skirt of a woman's gown — afire. With Stretch at his heels, Larry stumbled to the celldoor to gasp a warning.

He could have saved his breath. She was already reacting, dropping to the floor, rolling back and forth to smother the flames. Then she was on her feet and, with a sudden surge of hope, the Texans saw what she held in her right hand, a ring of keys. It was scarfaced Belle, hair dishevelled, eyes red from the smoke, or maybe from weeping.

'Do your damnedest — make it the right one!' pleaded Stretch.

At her third attempt, she jabbed the right key into the lock and turned it. The door swung open and, as they barged into the passage, Larry to wrap an arm around her, two blazing planks and other burning debris fell. To the connecting door they moved as fast as their legs could work to find most of the office as yet intact; the firebrand must have fallen only on the rear section of the roof. Larry at once took the key-ring from the woman and hunkered by the safe, while Stretch took their sidearms from the gunrack.

'Hurry!' she panted.

'It'll be the littlest key,' muttered Larry. 'Yeah, this's the one.'

He unlocked the safe. From it he took his watch, Stretch's harmonica and their jack-knives. With the woman gripping his arm and Stretch following, he hurried to the outer doorway. Then they were in the centre of the street, the only smoke-free section of it, gulping air and studying the havoc.

It seemed every building lining the street was afire. A short distance from the county jail, Larry sighted a bundle wrapped in what looked to be bed linen.

'Dorrie,' Belle said wearily, 'She died — just before they started setting the fires. I could see them from the window.' Gesturing helplessly, she murmured, 'I had to — just set her down there — not on the sidewalk.'

Not on the sidewalk. Being of sun-dried plank, they too were ablaze. And now, as the drifters strapped on their Colts, Stretch tensed.

'The livery, runt! If Toone — didn't

think to turn our horses loose . . . !'

'Why would he?' growled Larry, beginning his run. 'They were expectin' a raid. They couldn't know the town was gonna burn.'

The barn happened to be the last building set afire. When the tall men barged in, it was smoke-filled, the roof and hayloft afire and, in adjoining stalls, the sorrel and pinto nickering shrilly, pounding to be let out. Larry gave himself the risky chore of freeing the fear-crazed animals, daring their flailing hooves, while Stretch bee-lined for where their gear had been dumped. The horses ran for the street doorway. Larry sidestepped to join his partner and, together, they emerged from the barn hefting saddles and harnesses, packrolls, sheathed Winchesters and saddlebags.

Belle approached as they dumped their burdens in the middle of the street. She voiced a plea to men who weren't about to refuse her. Then and there, she could have demanded anything of them, their prized horses, their weapons, anything; no limit to the gratitude of men who, but for her endangering her own life would now be charred bodies in what remained of the jailhouse.

'Will you help me bury Dorrie? I'd never ask any Curran man — especially Bart Hanslow. He called her just a whore — and the others didn't understand her anyway. Maybe you can find tools — spades — a pickaxe?'

'We'll do it,' Larry assured her. 'Lady, after what you did for us, you couldn't ask anything we wouldn't do for you.'

'Heard us hollerin', huh?' prodded Stretch.

'No,' she said. 'It was just a guess. Any hint of real trouble, men like Billy Ackers, Sam Phipps and Hanslow would be first to make a run for it, thinking only of their own skins. Maybe they remembered you, but that wouldn't make any difference to them.' She turned to study the burning structures flanking the street. 'Carpenter's shop's going up in smoke, so there'll be no coffin for Dorrie nor any lumber for making one. It doesn't matter. Her poor little body can stay wrapped in those bedclothes.'

Later, the Texans would spare a thought for their horses. The sorrel and pinto had fled out of scent of fire and smoke. As was their way, they would return, looking for their masters, soon enough.

Stretch found an undamaged spade and pickaxe. Larry gathered the body in his arms and, with the scarred woman, they trudged to the tiny cemetery. It and the schoolhouse and chapel were the only Curran places spared by the arsonists. They found space near the summit of the gentle hill west of town dotted with crosses and headstones. Larry lowered the pitiful bundle to soft grass and, as he and his partner began digging, put a question to Belle. How much had she seen from that window?

'I've never seen soldiers do what they did,' she said bitterly. 'And I don't believe Curran was in danger. If half-breed raiders, a big force, had already crossed the border and were headed this way, they'd have over-run the town long before now. So it was all a lie, a trick that sent everybody running — everybody who could. You were trapped and — I had to stay too. She was my friend. You don't run out on a friend.'

'Had 'emselves a lootin spree?' Stretch asked while shovelling.

'I saw one of them bring something out of the emporium just before they started setting fire to everything,' she said. 'Looked like a metal box — about so big.' She spread her hands. 'He secured it to his horse while the others were fixing and throwing firebrands and gathering brush and packing it against walls. Eight soldiers — all of them laughing.'

Larry swung the pickaxe again and suppressed the urge to curse.

'At least one of 'em heard us yellin',' he told her. 'We figured we were goners, begged to be set free.'

'And — he didn't . . . ?' she began.

'He laughed,' Larry recalled.

'Said stay and fry,' mumbled Stretch. 'Him we'll remember.'

'If we ever catch up with him, that'll be the worst day of his life,' declared Larry. He paused to draw a sleeve across his face. 'What'd she die of, Belle?'

'She'd been around South Arizona and this territory too long,' sighed Belle. 'The alkali dust — bad for puny people with weak lungs.'

'Sick a long time,' guessed Stretch.

'She was coughing blood just before her heart stopped,' said Belle.

Larry's nerves were still jangled by a recent ordeal and by this sorry scene being enacted in Curran's cemetery. The woman's solemn eyes were following their every movement. He felt this was painful for her and, to distract her, asked bluntly, 'Who did

44

that to your face?'

'A Bar Five cowhand crazy drunk.' She answered him just as bluntly. 'Did it with a broken bottle. And no, Billy Ackers didn't arrest him. A week later, that cowhand's horse threw him. He hit a rock by the trail head-first and that was the death of him. If that hadn't happened, I'd have killed him myself. I was just waiting my chance.'

She answered other questions until the grave was six feet deep, recalling seeing the safe carried out of Sperlman's bank during the exodus, children being fetched from school and placed in wagons. It had been a fast evacuation.

As gently as possible, the tall men lowered the wrapped body into the grave. Larry matched stares with Belle a moment.

'You want to say anything over her?' he asked. 'A prayer or somethin'?'

She nodded. The Texans bared their heads as she began intoning a psalm — after a mumbled apology.

'Sorry, Dorrie. I'll try, but I mightn't

get all the words right.'

Stretch hesitated a moment before fishing out his harmonica. He played 'Rock Of Ages' softly while the scarred woman did her best.

'The Lord is my shepherd, I shall not want. He maketh me to lie down in green pastures. He hath brought unto me the water of refreshment and converted my soul. He hath led me on the path of righteousness for his Name's sake. Yea, though I walk in the shadow of death I will fear no evil, for Thou art with me. Thy rod and Thy staff have comforted me . . . ' She bowed her head. 'That's all I remember.'

Stretch pocketed his harmonica and shrugged uncomfortably. She bent, took a handful of earth from the heap and let it fall into the grave, after which the tall men took turns to wield the spade. When the grave was filled in, she stared at the mound and told them, 'I'll fix some kind of marker first chance I get. Thank you, Mister Valentine. You too,

Mister Emerson.'

'Know us, huh?' frowned Stretch. She nodded. 'Yeah, well, we owe you our hides, so don't never call us Mister. He's Larry to you. I'm Stretch.'

'I'm Belle Fassen,' she offered.

'At Hanslow's, anybody else recognize us?' demanded Larry.

'They couldn't have — certainly not Hanslow and his plug-ugly friends,' she said. 'Otherwise they wouldn't have had the nerve to try pushing you around, even though you looked dead on your feet. No, only three of us know who you are.'

'Who're the other two?' asked Larry.

'Zack and Carrie Dryden who run the general store,' she replied. 'The only two citizens who've been kind to me. We, meaning just the three of us, saw your pictures in newspapers some time or other I guess.'

'Who do we thank for the chow?' frowned Stretch.

'It was me pushed it through your window,' she said. 'But who do you suppose supplied it?'

'Before we quit this territory, there's a thing or two we got to do,' said Larry.

'Includin' rememberin' to thank the Drydens,' nodded Stretch.

'Something else,' said Belle. And with her gown a blackened wreck and most of one leg exposed, it did not embarrass her to delve into her cleavage and produce an item very familiar to both drifters, Larry's hip-wallet. As she handed it to him, she calmly explained, 'I got my hand to it when the brawl was just starting. Nobody noticed. They were all set to beat up on you, so it was my best chance. I don't know how much is in there, haven't even opened it. But, if you want to count it . . .'

'I don't want to count it,' muttered Larry.

'Doggone it, runt, we're beholden,' declared Stretch.

'And then some,' agreed Larry.

'Saved us from starvin', saved our

lives and our bankroll too.' Stretch eyed her gratefully and with respect. 'We sure owe you, Belle.'

'Whatever you had, it's just ash now,' Larry assumed.

'There wasn't time for any packing,' she shrugged. 'After Dorrie died and I heard the troopers riding east, I heard the fires too. Hanslow's started to burn and the only thing I could do was wrap Dorrie and carry her out of there. It wasn't till I was in Main Street that — I wondered if those chicken-livered lawmen had thought to set you free.'

'So you came a'runnin',' said Larry. 'And, if you hadn't, we wouldn't got out alive.'

'Don't think of giving me money,' she murmured as he opened his wallet. 'You heroes are the only two I can recall walking into that bar-room and tipping your hats to me. That meant a lot to me, so forget about paying . . .'

'Listen now, we know you got pride and we admire you for it,' he said earnestly. 'But look at this our way. How much're our lives worth? Damn it, Belle, you're entitled to every dollar we got.'

'The whole walletful,' insisted Stretch.

'No,' she said.

Larry changed his tactics, aiming his pitch at the sorry state of the clothes she stood in, demanding she at least accept cash enough to cover herself decently. She felt at her torn and blackened gown and winced. Then, as he slid a bill from the wallet, she shook her head and protested again.

'No, that's too much anyway, a fifty dollar bill.'

'Smoke must've got to your eyes,' he countered. 'I'm foldin' two fifties. If you won't take our whole bankroll, you're gonna take this much — even if I have to do it the hard way. Is that how it has to be, Belle? You gonna make me stash this dinero where you had my wallet hid?'

She matched stares with him a long moment, her eyes reading him. With the vaguest hint of a smile, almost imperceptible, she remarked, 'I think doing that would embarrass you more than it would embarrass me. So I'll accept the hundred — with thanks.'

'Listen to who's thankin' us,' Stretch muttered as she took the money from Larry. 'After all she did, after all we owe her.'

'I won't ask what's next,' she said, as they left the cemetery. 'Already guessed you'll saddle up and pursue those soldiers.'

'Got other chores first,' said Larry. 'But we'll be bird-doggin' 'em soon enough.'

'Somebody got to find the townfolk and hand 'em some real mean news,' said Stretch. 'And, far as we know, our horses're the only critters left in Curran.'

'You mean what's left of Curran,' she said grimly.

The tall men whistled shrilly while re-entering the street with Belle Fassen. A few moments later, the sorrel and pinto plodded into view.

'We ain't leavin' you in a burned out town all by your lonesome,' Larry told Belle. 'You'll ride double with me, and we'll be fetchin' you back as well.'

Calmer now, the horses submitted to saddling. The Texans secured packrolls, saddlebags and rifles and, after Stretch swung astride his pinto, Larry boosted the woman onto his sorrel and swung up behind her.

'North,' she said, and they headed in that direction.

Finding their way to Guillermo Canyon was pitifully easy, thanks to the tracks left by Curran's panic-stricken population. Larry had thought to rewind and set his watch to a rough estimate of the time of day. On his reckoning, it was some ten minutes after high noon when, in the distance, they sighted the canyon entrance, the people crowding it and the nine horsemen sitting their mounts nearby. Larry promptly fished his field-glasses from a saddlebag and urged Belle use them.

'The riders, who are they?'

After training the glasses on the horsemen, she replied, 'They'd be Half Circle men. The one on the dun stallion is Caleb Bassault. He owns Half Circle. It's a big ranch and — I know what you'll ask next — the answer is no. He's no admirer of Hanslow nor those buzzards we call lawmen.'

She returned the binoculars to the saddlebag. As they drew closer, Stretch said contemptuously, 'I see 'em.'

'I see 'em too,' said Larry. 'But we don't settle our score with 'em till we're through explainin' things to the townsfolks.'

'That will cause a lot of grief,' declared Belle. 'But you're in no way to blame and they have to be told.'

Now that they were close enough to be recognized, they heard themselves named.

'Belle Fassen!' exclaimed the storekeeper.

'I wondered where she was,' frowned his wife.

'Hey, Billy!' cried Phipps. 'Them saddlebums've broke jail!'

'You'll try to arrest them again?' Dryden sourly challenged. 'No, I wouldn't think so. You don't have your shot-guns now.'

The Texans reined up. The Half Circle boss addressed them authoritatively.

'Smoke's visible from here. You've come to tell us those Armendariz raiders set fires?'

'You're Caleb Bassault.' Larry made it a statement, not a question, but the lean and leathery rancher nodded anyway. 'All right now, Valentine's my handle and this here's my partner — name of Emerson. We got no quarrel with you or any of your hired hands, so what d'you say we keep it that way?'

Bassault met his gaze a moment, grinned briefly and glanced at Ackers and Phipps, who appeared stunned.

'Fine by me, Valentine,' he drawled.

'But, from the looks of our brave lawmen, I'd say they got a quarrel — and they're wishing they never started it.'

'Before today, did you ever hear of a bossbandido name of Armendariz?' demanded Larry.

'Don't believe I ever did,' said Bassault. He turned in his saddle to challenge his crew. 'Any of you?'

'Border raiders — big outfit,' said Larry.

'About sixty of 'em,' said Stretch.

Plainly, no Half Circle man had ever heard of Armendariz. Larry switched his attention to the Curran folk grouped in the canyon mouth. Gazing beyond them, Stretch noted the other people and the children, the circle of rigs of every kind.

'How about you folks?' asked Larry.

'I believe I speak for everybody,' frowned Sperlman. 'All we know of the Armendariz band is what we were told by Lieutenant Nolan of the Second Cavalry.'

'So — I'm sorry — but I got bad news for you,' said Larry. 'The soldiers made up Armendariz. Your town was in danger, but not from border raiders — just Nolan and his men. They spooked you into quittin' town.'

'It was a hoax?' gasped Seth Rowley, as his fellow-citizens recoiled in shock.

'Some trick,' commented Jake Toone. 'Some dirty trick.'

'But why would they . . . ?' began Sperlman.

'They burned Curran,' declared Belle.

'Miss Belle stayed to tend her friend Dorrie,' explained Larry. 'From a window, she saw what they . . . '

'*Miss* Belle?' jeered Hanslow. 'Hey, *that's* a joke!'

'Mister Emerson, suh,' Larry said grimly.

'Glad to oblige, Mister Valentine, suh,' muttered Stretch.

He dismounted and advanced on Hanslow, who made to retreat, but did not move fast enough. Stretch grasped a fistful of his shirtfront and backhanded him once, twice, thrice, then turned him and swung a kick to his backside, sending him sprawling on face and hands. The people gawked. Bassault and his men sat their mounts, watching, keeping their thoughts to themselves.

'Like I was sayin'',' Larry continued, 'Miss Belle saw the troopers burn Curran. One of 'em took some kind of tin box out of your store.' He looked at Dryden, who turned pale and began trembling. 'Seemed like the only thing they grabbed.'

The people began bewailing the destruction of their town. Stretch told them the only buildings spared were the school and church, while Bassault edged his mount closer to the sorrel to question Larry.

'You and your partner were in the county jail — and it burned too?'

'Them sonsabitches locked us up after a hassle at Hanslow's,' growled Larry, his cold eyes on the lawmen. 'They ran like everybody else . . .'

'They were first to run,' recalled Sperlman, coloring angrily.

'So we were stuck when the jail caught fire,' muttered Larry. 'Would've burned alive but for Belle. Right after her friend died, she toted her out of Hanslow's and saw the town afire and the troopers headed east. Then — she guessed Ackers'd just leave us there — and she came a'runnin' to turn us loose, near got herself killed doin' it.' Now he dismounted, scowling at Ackers and Phipps. 'You just quit and ran for it — you yellow-gutted polecats.'

'Damn you, Ackers, it was an evacuation!' snapped Sperlman. 'As sheriff, it was your responsibility to make sure *everybody* left! Yet two women were left behind, one of them critically ill — and two men locked in your jail!'

'Ain't much of anything left,' said Stretch.

'Includin' the jail.' Larry's eyes gleamed. 'Look at Belle's clothes and you'll savvy how we neared burned along with it.'

The people were moving back to vehicles and saddle-animals, anxious to travel home and see for themselves what eight rogues had done to their town. Ackers and Phipps began moving, but were intercepted by two trouble-shooters in the grip of fury and disgust. Bassault signalled his hired hands to stay in their saddles. The cattlemen watched, none protesting, when the sheriff was belly-punched by Larry and thrown on his back by a savage right to the jaw. At Stretch's hands, and despite his efforts to defend himself, Phipps suffered similar punishment. Both lawmen were down and bloody and groaning when the Texans remounted.

'What'll you do now?' asked Bassault.

'Back to Curran, but just to fill our canteens,' Larry told him. 'Then we'll be headed east.'

'We got a score to settle with the army,' scowled Stretch. 'One of 'em heard us hollerin' while the calaboose burned — hollerin' and beggin' to be set free.'

'You *sure* he heard you?' frowned Bassault.

'We're sure,' growled Larry. 'And we ain't about to forget what *he* hollered at us. Stay and fry.'

'And he was laughin',' said Stretch.

'Hell,' breathed the rancher. 'So it's personal with you, and I sure don't blame you. Sorry I can't spare any of my men, otherwise I'd send some of 'em along with you. But anything else I can do . . . '

'There's somethin',' sighed Stretch. 'We used up our Bull Durham better'n a week ago — can't remember our last smoke.'

The reaction of the Half Circle riders was generous and prompt. Men fished out Durham sacks and matches and tossed them. The Texans indicated their gratitude and wheeled their mounts.

Belle, they observed, had accepted a lift home from the Drydens and was huddled behind the driver's seat. The other rigs were rolling and mounted townmen hustling past when the storekeeper beckoned them. They veered to ride level with the Dryden wagon.

'I heard what you told Caleb, so I understand and — and acknowledge your right to avenge yourselves.' He was haggard, his voice shaky with emotion. 'But before you begin hunting those rogue-troopers — there's something I want to ask of you. Terribly important to me — and to Carrie here. Will you wait long enough to listen to my plea?'

'No way we could refuse you, friend,' frowned Larry. 'But for you folks — and Belle — my partner and me could've starved in that stinkin' jail.'

'Little enough to do,' Carrie said dolefully.

'Meant a lot to us, ma'am,' muttered Stretch.

'So you don't have to hold back from askin' a favor,' Larry assured Dryden.

'I'm clinging to the hope I won't

have to ask,' said the storekeeper. 'But I fear I'll — have no choice.'

The homecoming was traumatic for the townfolk. Curran was a smoldering shambles now. Some of the homes east and west of town had, like the school-house and the church, been spared. Karl Sperlman's was one of these, but he was as irate as his fellow-citizens. His bank had burned. He could only give thanks he had ordered the removal of the safe; at least his clients would not be impoverished. He stared toward the Dryden wagon and shook his head sadly.

Dryden stalled his rig in front of the little that remained of his place of business these past twenty years, helped his wife down and politely requested Belle take care of her.

'This is something — I have to find out for myself,' he said before stumbling away through the debris.

As they led their horses to the well near the gutted livery stable, the Texans noticed the banker hurrying after Dryden. Carrie stood by the wagon with Belle Fassen's arm about her, sobbing.

Sperlman came upon Dryden in the ruin of the small structure out back; it used to serve as bathhouse and laundry. Being made of rock slabs, the floor had survived. One slab had been raised and shoved aside. With Dryden, the banker gazed into the cavity.

'This was it, Zack?' he asked quietly. 'This was where you kept your life savings hidden rather than open an account at my bank?'

'All our cash, save what's in my pockets and Carrie's purse,' groaned Dryden. 'And something else — an heirloom — of great value.'

'Zack, I'm most sincerely sorry for you,' muttered Sperlman. 'In this time of distress, I won't make it worse by reminding you . . . '

'You warned me time and time again,' mumbled Dryden. 'But — I could never forget the great loss suffered by my cousin.'

'Yes, you told me of your cousin — every time I tried to persuade you to entrust your savings to me,' nodded Sperlman. 'No fools like old fools? Well, I've been just as foolish. I too have learned a harsh lesson this day. I'll be approaching an insurance company as soon as possible.'

'It's more tragic than you know, Karl,' sighed Dryden. 'There's an even greater loss.'

'There is?' said Sperlman.

'Yes, but I'll explain later,' said Dryden. 'I must talk to — the only men who can do anything about it — before they leave.'

The drifters had filled their canteens and were awaiting him by the well, relishing the sensation of rolling cigarettes.

'Look at the poor old sonofagun,' Stretch said softly. 'Wiped out.'

'Whatever he wants from us, he'll get it,' decided Larry.

3

Destination Camp Selburn

THEY smoked while listening to Zack Dryden's plea. He seemed familiar with their reputation; why else would he take them into his confidence to this extent?

'I know it's inevitable,' he began. 'You'll find those thieves . . . '

'No matter how long it takes, old-timer, or how far the hunt takes us,' Stretch grimly assured him.

'And it's bound to end in violence — there'll be bloodshed,' muttered Dryden. 'But my wife and I would be forever grateful if you could take at least one of them alive.'

'We're plenty sore, but we ain't kill-crazy,' said Larry. 'Give us a chance and we'd as soon take all eight of 'em alive. It's just . . . ' He shrugged and

65

grimaced, 'I don't look for that kind of trash to surrender peaceful. You said it, Mister Dryden. It's almost for sure there'll be shootin'.'

'You'll try, you'll at least try?' begged Dryden. 'Just one — so that he can be questioned?'

'If we can,' nodded Larry. 'Took you for everything, did they?'

'My own fault — maybe.' The storekeeper's aversion to the banking system was explained in detail. A bank had been looted in a Kansas town long years before. His cousin, a baker, had been a depositor and, like all the bank's clients, had lost his life savings; it had been an independent bank, not a branch of a big chain, and uninsured. 'Poor Frank's misfortune shocked me as you might imagine, left a lasting impression? Knowing Karl Sperlman carried no insurance, I refused to entrust my cash to him. I kept it hidden in a large metal box, confident no thief could ever find it.'

'Good hideaway, huh?' prodded Stretch.

'Each week, I'd convert all small bills and coins to hundred dollar bills at the bank,' Dryden told them. 'Every time I took cash to the hiding place, anybody who noticed me would take it for granted I was going to shave or bathe. The little place behind the store — do you understand? Bathhouse and laundry. The floor is of stone slabs.'

'Your stash was under one of them slabs,' guessed Larry.

'And just our secret,' declared Dryden. 'Only three of us knew of it, meaning Carrie and me — but not our daughter. Harriet was never curious about it. She was going to school and — thank God she's safe and far from here now, married to the Western Union man in Phoenix.'

'So who's the third party?' asked Larry.

'Our nephew, Todd Melrose, only son of my dear sister and her husband who died within a few months of each other some ten years ago,' said Dryden. 'Todd's a decent, honorable man. He was like a son to us, spent quite some time here. He helped in the store and, naturally, he knew how I kept our money safe. When he could see — well — the years catch up with us, don't they? When he could see I was having difficulty lifting that slab, he'd take care of it for me.' He was suddenly grasping Larry's arm. 'Now do you understand? Only from Todd could they have learned of my hiding place, and only by torturing him! I haven't said this to Carrie, but I'm resigned to his death.'

'They wouldn't leave a live witness behind,' sighed Stretch.

'One of 'em must've hung around Curran a while,' mused Larry. 'Well, long enough to notice the only storekeeper in town never went into the bank. That'd get any thief interested.'

'It's the only explanation,' Dryden said dejectedly. 'We can learn to live with our great loss, not just the cash, but the heirloom . . . '

'The what?' frowned Stretch.

'Willed to Carrie by an old aunt of hers,' said Dryden. 'A necklace of great value. Rubies and emeralds. Carrie wouldn't think of wearing it — ever. She meant for our daughter to have it. That bequest is stipulated in Carrie's will. All right, we'll never see it again and — we can abide that loss — but . . . ' He bowed his head and began trembling again. The tall men winced uncomfortably. Larry tried clamping a hand to a shaking shoulder. 'But — what I can't bear the thought of — what will haunt me — is never knowing if poor Todd was given — any kind of burial. I have to know about that!'

'Yeah, well . . . ' began Larry.

'That's why you must take at least one of them alive — and force the truth from him!' panted Dryden. 'I want for Todd's body to be found and — if those bastards just — abandoned him in some lonely place . . . !'

69

'You don't have to say any more,' Larry said soothingly. 'You got our word, Mister Dryden. We'll make sure — either way.'

'If we have to bury him, we'll do it right,' promised Stretch.

'I guess . . . ' Larry hated to say it, but the question could not be avoided. 'Look, we'll have to be sure we've found the right man. Maybe you got a picture of him?' The storekeeper sadly shook his head. 'Well, what kind of a lookin' feller is he?'

'You mean was,' sighed Dryden.

'Sorry,' said Larry.

Dryden worked up a wistful smile, remembering.

'Tall, well-built, aged around thirty-two — maybe thirty-three. A handsome young man, always neat. Dark hair. Clear blue eyes and — the look of a man you at once trust. Fine character.'

'That gives us a general notion, runt,' remarked Stretch.

'I almost forgot,' said Dryden. He fished out a handkerchief to mop his brow. 'There's a distinctive mark that will positively identify the body . . . ' He faltered again. 'Depending on — its condition when you find it. A birthmark — brown — on the back of his left hand. A round spot, perfect circle, about the size of a quarter. Yes, a twenty-five cent coin.'

'That's enough,' Larry said gently. 'Better not talk any more, Mister Dryden. We'll be on our way now, and you better get back to your wife. And, listen, maybe the local doc's got brandy. You need a stiff shot.'

'It's all right,' said Dryden, turning away. 'I have *some* consolation now — knowing you're men of your word and that — you'll try to do as I've asked.'

They watched him trudge back to the wagon in front of his gutted store. Grim-visaged, they got mounted and turned their animals toward Curran's east side, and now they saw Belle Fassen again. She stood arms akimbo, eyes flashing as she addressed a flabby townman cringing from her. She wasn't raising her voice, but it was all too obvious she had no kind words for this red-nosed local.

Giving in to curiosity, they reined up beside the couple.

'Dorrie coughing her life away!' she fumed. 'You — who call yourself a doctor, a healer — running like the rest of them.' Suddenly aware of the Texans, she pointed to the object of her wrath. 'This is Ethan Clumm. A doctor — if you can believe it.'

'Nothin' I could do for your friend anyway,' mumbled Clumm. 'No cure for what killed her, and I got other folks countin' on me. Had to stay with the people. Damn it, Mamie Ingram's second's due any time.'

He couldn't look the tall riders in the eye. Head down, he skulked away. Belle then shrugged impatiently and gestured eastward.

'Eight, don't forget,' she offered. 'One an officer. You'll pick up their tracks.'

'Count on it, Belle,' said Larry. 'We ain't forgettin' *anything*.'

'Specially what you did for us,' declared Stretch.

'So do something for yourselves now,' she urged. 'Run them to ground, make them pay, but be careful. It would all be for nothing if you let them see you coming — and they ambushed you.'

'Don't worry,' said Larry. 'When they see us, it won't be till we want 'em to.'

They doffed their Stetsons to her and nudged their mounts to movement. East of devastated Curran, they easily cut sign of eight riders and began dogging them. They talked, but with their eyes busy; the open terrain ahead was kept under close observation.

Stretch rarely resorted to sarcasm, but he was still seething.

'I just hope the army's proud of 'em,' he scowled. 'Fine soldiers, huh? Credit to the U.S. Cavalry.'

'Rotten apples in many a barrel, Stretch,' muttered Larry. 'The big shots that boss big towns, the law, the army too.'

After two more miles, Stretch moodily announced, 'I've been thinkin'.'

'Keep doin' that,' advised Larry. 'It can be useful.'

'About Zack Dryden I mean,' said Stretch. 'I'd like it fine if, as well as nailin' them looters, we got back what they stole from the old feller, his dinero, his wife's purty jewels, everything. Be a good feelin', huh? Handin' it back to him?'

'I had the same idea,' said Larry. 'But what matters most is we should hold to our promise. Zack won't rest easy till he knows Todd Melrose got proper burial.'

'He's got to be right,' reflected Stretch. 'No other way they could know about his stash. They made Todd tell 'em.'

'Knife at his throat or a cocked gun at his head,' growled Larry. 'I don't blame the poor sonofagun for losin' his nerve.'

'Findin' his carcass mightn't be easy,' Stretch warned. 'They could've weighted it with rocks and dumped it in a river.'

'Whatever they did,' vowed Larry, 'one of 'em's gonna tell us.'

Their last meal was but a memory. For once, the taller trouble-shooter didn't complain of his growling belly. They hadn't arrived in Curran low on rations, were carrying enough for two, maybe three meals, but would stay hungry till sundown, so intent were they on keeping track of their quarry. As was his way, Stretch paused at intervals to collect such firewood as he could find, using his lariat to secure a sizeable bundle.

Thirty minutes before sundown, travelling higher country, they cursed bitterly, tugged their Stetsons lower over their brows and pulled up their bandanas to mask noses and mouths. The big blow began suddenly and they were riding right into it. Men and horses were bedeviled by dust and the powerful wind sweeping all hoofprints.

'Us and our lousy luck,' grouched Stretch.

In poor visibility, they searched for shelter and, just before the sun set, they came upon what they needed and heaved sighs of relief. The dark half circle at the base of a rocky rise proved to be a cave and spacious. Their horses could shelter with them.

They offsaddled the animals and, while Larry saw to their comfort, Stretch broke out provisions and got a fire going. It would be a rough but welcome supper, cans of beans, pork and tomatoes emptied into a pan, the pan set on the fire with the coffeepot.

During that meal, they speculated as to how soon Curran people would begin the chore of rebuilding their town.

'Lumber costs,' Stretch pointed out.

'When we see Curran again, we'll see more adobe than timber,' opined Larry. 'Adobe comes cheap. I think the banker, Sperlman, will help out with loans. And there's Bassault. Plenty he could do for the townfolk.'

'I wonder if that sonofabitch Hanslow'll build another still, get back in business again,' mused Stretch. 'And d'you suppose, when we come back, we'll find the same sheriff, the same deputy?'

'If Ackers and Phipps're still totin' badges, Curran deserves 'em,' Larry said coldly.

Their hunger satisfied, the coffeepot empty, they rolled and lit cigarettes. Stretch rose, moved to the cave entrance to listen to the wailing wind and watch the swirling dust.

'No tracks left for us to follow tomorrow,' he warned. 'What'll we do? Make straight for Camp Selburn? In Curran, they told us its northeast. Oughtn't be hard to find.'

'If it's still blowin' come sun-up, we'll try for the Second Cavalry camp,' Larry decided after pondering the question. 'But, if the wind's quit by then, we ought to split up an hour or two, scout around, look for more sign.'

'They probably headed straight back to where they came from,' suggested Stretch.

'Probably,' nodded Larry. 'But it won't do no harm to make sure.'

They bedded down early, surrendering to exhaustion. Case-hardened though they were, survivors of more crises than they could tally, this day had made inroads on their nervous systems and their physical strength. Their ordeal in a burning jail would not be forgotten. After that, their grave-digging chore, then the journey to Guillermo Canyon and the venting of their rage on lawmen unworthy of the badges they wore. Not one of their best days.

They slept deeply while, beyond their shelter, the wind persisted until around 4 a.m. The early sun roused them. They used part of the contents of their canteens to water their horses, shave and brew enough coffee for a cup apiece and, after a quick breakfast, killed the fire and got moving again.

A mile and a half farther east and

beyond a range of hills, they separated to search for tracks, Larry veering away to the north, Stretch southward.

It was mid-morning when Larry heard his partner's summons, the familiar rebel yell. He abandoned his own fruitless search and hustled the sorrel southward across flat terrain. In the distance, Stretch rose in his stirrups, the better to draw his attention. He headed that way to find his sidekick sitting his mount at the near rim of a basin; en route, he crossed the tracks found by Stretch.

'Same bunch for sure, all eight of 'em,' he was told when he reined up. 'They lead down to the basin floor, and you can see what happened down there.'

Larry noted the blackened area and nodded.

'Uh huh. Had 'emselves a fire, and not just for cookin' up some grub.'

'I looked all round 'fore I called you in,' said Stretch. 'No more sign, runt. From here, they split up, every rider draggin' somethin' to kill his back-trail. Or they're still together and the tag riders're draggin' brush, blankets, whatever. Plain enough they didn't hanker to be bird-dogged no farther.'

'Plain enough,' agreed Larry. 'So we head for Camp Selburn, but not till we do some snoopin' down there.'

They made a slow descent to the basin floor and dismounted. At once, Larry's hunch was confirmed. Maybe their quarry had cooked and eaten a meal here, but more than firewood had been burned. Stretch was moved to remark, as his partner hunkered and began prodding in the ashes with the remnant of a piece of firewood, 'Maybe you should've said yes.'

'Howzat again?' asked Larry, still probing.

'A lot of years ago, when the Pinkertons made you an offer,' said Stretch. 'You turned 'em down — on account of me — but you could've been one helluva detective, runt. That's how you think at a time like this. Like a regular sure enough detective.'

'They wanted me, not both of us, just me,' Larry recalled. 'That would've meant a split, you goin' your way, me goin' mine. A split — and the worst mistake of our lives.' He left off probing long enough to build a smoke. Stretch followed his example. They lit up and matched stares. 'Real bad mistake, amigo. Think of how many tight fixes we fought our way out of since way back then. If either of us'd been goin' it alone, we'd be long dead.'

'Well, come to think of it . . . ' Stretch reminisced, 'you've saved my hide many a time since then.'

'About as often as you've saved mine,' said Larry. 'It's been twenty years . . . '

'Longer'n that,' drawled Stretch.

' . . . and we're stuck with each other,' declared Larry. 'We near died in that Curran jail, near got ourselves killed many another time. The way is adds up, stringbean, only reason we're still alive is we're still together.'

'Helluva way to live,' suggested Stretch.

'Beats bein' dead,' retorted Larry.

'Ain't that the truth,' shrugged Stretch.

He reached for a stick and joined Larry in investigating the embers and ash. A few moments later, Larry delved with finger and thumb, salvaged something small, blew ash from it, then rubbed it against his shirtsleeve for a closer inspection. Almost simultaneously, Stretch extricated something, about seven inches of fabric, a triangle of it, its edges charred. He held it out to Larry, who glanced at it and observed,

'Blue. Cavalry blue, I'd reckon.'

'What've you got?' asked Stretch, squinting.

'Button,' said Larry. He held it close to Stretch's face. 'Take a good close look.'

'Off of a uniform,' opined Stretch. 'How about that? They burned their outfits here?'

'Everything 'cept a button and a piece of cloth,' nodded Larry. 'And maybe that'll be enough.'

'Enough for what?' prodded Stretch.

'To convince the boss-officer at Selburn he's got eight rotten apples in his barrel,' said Larry. He took the triangle of cloth from Stretch and pocketed it along with the button. 'Best get movin' again.'

'Push east,' Stretch guessed as they remounted. 'Look for a trail. Has to be a trail somewheres, if Selburn's a regular settlement.'

In the early afternoon, a short time after watering their horses by the east bank of the Gila River and refilling their canteens, they studied the clear shallows and traded glances. It seemed a long time since their last all-over bath, and their clothes were filthy and giving off an odor to remind them of their near death in a blazing calaboose. There was no discussion; the decision was mutual. In this heat, their garments would dry fast. They could spread them on rocks or use a lariat to makeshift a line.

And so they broke out soap, tugged off Stetsons and boots, removed pants, belts and sidearms, emptied their pockets and flopped in the shallows to strip. They rubbed grime from underwear and outer garments, soaped and rinsed them, then gave their battle-scarred bodies the same treatment.

Squatting naked on the bank, waiting for their clothes to dry, they smoked and discussed their chances of apprehending the men they sought without having to do battle with the whole Second Cavalry Regiment.

'We don't have a description worth a damn of the bastards we're huntin',' remarked Larry. 'On the other hand, they didn't get a look at us.'

'We just heard one of 'em — him that laughed,' growled Stretch.

'A voice and a laugh I'll remember,' Larry said softly. 'Kind of a gurglin' laugh.'

'So what do we do?' asked Stretch.

'Little private parley with a noncom — to find out which eight hombres've been gone from camp a while?'

'How do we know one of 'em wasn't a noncom, them that burned Curran and grabbed Dryden's fortune?' countered Larry. 'Why d'you suppose they got rid of their outfits in that hollow? It figures they left other uniforms stashed there.'

'Could've been officers in on it,' frowned Stretch.

'What it gets down to is there's only one soldier we ought to parley with,' insisted Larry. 'Only safe one'd be the boss himself. I mean the big boss. Ain't likely he was in on it.'

'The C.O.?' blinked Stretch. 'Hell, he could be a general. How do we reach such a big shot? You think a guard'd let us sashay right into his office?'

'We'll fret about that when we get there,' decided Larry.

★ ★ ★

They found a trail, also a crossroads with a signpost that pointed them to their destination. 2.30 of the following afternoon, they sighted the township, but paid it little attention at first. Selburn was no small town; however they were more interested in the lines of tents west of it, the flagpole from which Old Glory fluttered and the little they could see of the adobe and log administration block.

The sentry to whom they put their request eyed them dubiously and scratched his head.

'You want to talk to Colonel Bostwick himself? Would he know you?'

'We never had the pleasure, friend,' said Larry. 'But it could be he's heard of us. Try anyway, huh? We don't care how long we got to wait. Can you get a message to him?'

'Guess so. Who wants to see him?'

'The names're Valentine and Emerson. And we wouldn't be botherin' him if it wasn't important — meanin' *mighty* important.'

The sentry passed the word along. Ten minutes passed before a reply was received. The visitors were directed to the hitchrail fronting the administration block and, while headed there, won little attention from off duty troopers. When they were dismounting and looping their reins, the orderly officer emerged.

'Valentine and Emerson?' he frowned.

'That's us, suh,' nodded Stretch.

'The colonel has agreed to see you,' said the officer. 'I'll take you to his office.'

The tall men followed the orderly officer inside and, spurs jingling, through an outer office and along a short corridor to a closed door. After knocking and entering, the officer reappeared.

'You can go in now.'

He closed the door behind them after they crossed the threshold, nodded respectfully to the grey-mustached C.O. and bared their heads. For a long moment, and through shrewd brown eyes, he contemplated them. Colonel

Henry Bostwick's close-cropped thatch matched the mustache. He was distinguished-looking, a veteran ageing handsomely and, right now, full of curiosity. This he at once admitted.

'Only my curiosity prompted me to grant this interview. I wanted to look you over and decide for myself if you really are larger than life.'

'Runt,' winced Stretch. 'He's heard of us.'

'Guess we ought to beg your pardon, Colonel,' Larry diplomatically suggested. 'You'd have to be the busiest officer of this whole outfit, so your time's valuable.'

'Nice touch of courtesy there,' approved Bostwick. 'Well, so you're the tearaway Texans who've been bandit-fighters since long before I became a major. Now I've had another promotion . . .'

'Congratulations,' offered Stretch.

'And the years pass and some of us grow older,' Bostwick continued with a half-grin, 'while some of us — well, two of us — appear to be defying the ageing process. Be seated, gentlemen, and answer a question I've no doubt you're weary of hearing.' They sank into the chairs fronting his desk. 'The question is: how in thunderation have you managed to survive your hundreds of battles with rustlers, outlaws and the like?'

Stretch was stuck for an explanation; he shrugged helplessly.

'Just lucky, I guess, Colonel suh.'

'We're only human,' Larry assured Bostwick. 'We've bled many a time and we got the scars to prove it.'

'Incredible,' frowned Bostwick. 'And now may I ask why you requested this interview rather than address your enquiries to some junior officer?'

'The way it stacks up, we figured it ought to be you,' said Larry. 'It'd be hard for us to believe the commandant of this regiment'd do what eight soldiers did to Curran.'

The colonel's eyebrows shot up.

'Who is Curran?'

'Not who — better you ask what,' said Larry. 'Little town a ways southwest of here, few miles north of the Mexico border.'

'Must be an insignificant place,' said Bostwick. He rose, revealing himself to be a shade under six feet and toting no excess fat, and moved to a wallmap. 'No, I don't see it. Nothing to indicate such a town exists.' He turned to face them again. 'Eight soldiers did what to Curran?'

Larry offered a terse but comprehensive account of Curran's day of disaster and, during his recounting each event, the colonel resumed his chair, lit a cigar and eyed him intently, not missing a word. When Larry had told it all, he flatly declared, 'There is no Lieutenant Martin Nolan in my command. The perpetrators of the outrage you've described must be impostors.' He frowned at the tip of his cigar and grimaced. 'Caesar's ghost. One of them heard you — and refused to release you from a burning jail.'

'One thing I figured — easily,' said Larry. 'There's no Armendariz gang of half-Apaches raisin' hell this side of the border.'

'Obviously not,' said Bostwick. 'Had such a raiding party been heard of, Second Cavalry patrols would be out hunting them. There are in fact no patrols out at this time. I keep my finger on the pulse of all Second Cavalry operations. Nothing affecting my regiment escapes my attention, Mister Valentine.'

Stretch shifted in his chair to challenge Larry.

'Fakers, runt? Only makin' believe they were soldiers?'

'The uniforms . . . ' began Larry.

'Don't even ask,' chided Bostwick. 'It would be impossible. But, if anything so unlikely occurred, the theft of eight uniforms from the Second's stores — one of them the uniform of a lieutenant — I'd have been immediately advised. See here, Valentine, I'm properly sympathetic. I'm appalled by the outrage suffered by the Curran community and the theft of the storekeeper's valuables and, if there were any way I could help, I'd certainly do so. And I certainly approve your determination to apprehend the men responsible.'

'Sure,' frowned Larry. 'Thanks.'

'Listen — uh — if they didn't lift them outfits from this regiment, maybe some other army post hereabouts,' suggested Stretch.

'The Second is the only regiment in this region,' retorted Bostwick. 'If you hold to your belief the uniforms were stolen from the army, you'd have to ask your questions farther afield, Fort Denning in fact. That's almost a two hundred mile journey north.'

'They burned their duds,' said Stretch.

'The uniforms?' challenged Bostwick. 'You're certain of that?'

'A ways east of Curran,' said Larry. 'We found the place, checked the ashes and this is what we dug out.'

He produced the button and triangle

of cloth and profferred them for Bostwick's inspection. Bostwick fingered the fabric, spared the button only a glance and called to the orderly officer.

'Quartermaster Sergeant Marrigan — on the double!'

In a matter of minutes, a bulky noncom knocked and entered, accorded the C.O. a smart salute and stood to attention.

'Colonel?'

'At ease, Marrigan,' said Bostwick. 'Your expert opinion, if you please.' He nodded to the items salvaged by his visitors. 'Examine them carefully. I want them identified, and who better than you?'

'Yes, sir,' nodded the sergeant. He picked up the articles, squinted and darted a glance to the window. 'With the colonel's permission . . . '

'Raise the shade higher,' Bostwick said impatiently. 'Give yourself ample light and, for heaven's sake, don't be self-conscious. I know you have

93

to use spectacles. So do I, and you can bet your stripes *I'm* not at all disconcerted. Damn it, Marrigan, we aren't youngsters any more. The years catch up.'

'Yes, sir,' said Marrigan. He moved to the window, raised the shade and donned spectacles. First he felt at the cloth, studying it closely. Then he fished out a bandana, wet the edge of it with his tongue and rubbed at the button, the better to inspect the design. A pause, then, 'The colonel has a question?'

'Need I put it into words?' growled Bostwick. 'You know the question.'

'Not army issue, sir,' declared Marrigan. 'Stake my life. The cloth's not the right weight. Same goes for the button. I've seen no such emblem on any button since I enlisted — cavalry, infantry, any part of the U.S. Army.'

'That will be all,' said Bostwick. 'Return the articles to this gentleman . . . ' He nodded to Larry. 'And thanks, Roy. Knew I could count on you.'

'Any time, Hank — I mean Colonel,' said Marrigan.

He passed the items to Larry. Bostwick returned his salute and then he was gone.

'Old barracks room buddies, Roy and me,' Bostwick confided. 'We fought side by side at Horrock's Ford in 'sixty-two as sassy troopers. Water under the bridge. One of us rose high from the ranks, one no higher than quartermaster sergeant.'

'Them's the breaks,' Larry said distractedly. 'Horrock's Ford? Yeah. We were in that one.'

'You have to accept Roy's findings,' said Bostwick. 'Take my word, he knows army equipment. The uniforms worn by those thieves *couldn't* have been genuine.'

'Well,' grouched Stretch. 'This is a fine howdy-do and the same to you. Doggone it, runt, we're near back where we started.'

'I can offer only one suggestion,' said Bostwick. 'It may help — or you may learn nothing. But at least you wouldn't have to travel any farther than Selburn's main street.'

'Muchas gracias,' said Larry. 'We're listenin'.'

'Onslow's tailor shop,' said Bostwick. 'Some officers — of awkward build for instance — prefer to have their uniforms made to measure. Tailors with that experience often establish themselves in proximity to an army post. Of course Onslow is obliged to use only regulation materials, but it's just possible he may give you a clue as to the origin of that button, maybe the cloth also.'

'Worth tryin', runt,' Stretch remarked, as they rose to leave.

'*Anything's* worth tryin',' muttered Larry. 'Thanks for your time, Colonel. We sure appreciate it.'

4

A Possible Clue

MOUNTED again and slow-walking their horses into the township, the Texans heard a hiss of steam and a locomotive's whistle. A freight train rolled south. So Selburn was on the railroad. This didn't seem important at the moment.

In their haste to reach the Second Cavalry's camp, they had skipped lunch. They stopped by a cafe to down a hearty meal, double servings of everything, before seeking the premises of J. T. Onslow, tailor to the gentry of Selburn and the U.S. Army. A local obliged with directions and, a short time later, they were tethering their mounts at a hitchrail some twenty-five yards from the Onslow store.

Onslow, a short, dapper, middle-aged man attended them personally. He didn't flinch when they informed him they were not in the market for new clothes and waxed co-operative when Larry explained, 'What we need's professional advice, in a manner of speakin'. It was Colonel Bostwick said we should look you up. Maybe you can help, maybe you can't.'

'So, gentlemen, let's find out, shall we?' the tailor suggested.

'We know this stuff ain't regular army issue,' said Larry, placing the button and cloth on the counter. 'What we're tryin' to find out is where it came from.'

Onslow's curiosity was aroused. He didn't rely entirely on his spectacles, but rummaged in a drawer and found a magnifying glass, and his examination was thorough. He held the piece of material up to the light, used the glass for a minute inspection of the button.

'All right,' he said finally. 'I can offer you a guess, and a good one. Actually, it's the most logical explanation. These articles are what's left of garments supplied by a theatrical costume company.'

Noting their puzzled stares, he elaborated, reminding them of the many repertory companies touring the West, some performing melodramas, some Shakespeare, some larger groups in which musicians were included, presenting Gilbert & Sullivan. Also, he stressed, melodramas of a military background were not uncommon.

'Hey now,' frowned Stretch.

'Maybe we're gettin' somewhere,' said Larry. 'Play-actors rigged up like soldiers?'

'A pageant for instance,' offered Onslow. 'Something like Lincoln's Gettysburg address. His audience would naturally include army personnel, so the producers would have to rent or purchase suitable costumes. That's why there have to be stores specializing in supplying such items.' For a few moments, he showed exasperation. 'A likelier possibility would be yet another play about Custer's Last Stand, usually very fanciful and highly inaccurate. I was foolish enough to attend a performance about three years ago. Gentlemen, I'm no cheapskate, but it was deplorable, so much so I almost demanded the return of the price of admission.'

'They didn't have to be regular play-actors,' Larry remarked to Stretch. 'And the uniforms looked genuine, could easily fool small town folks.' He looked at Onslow again. 'You happen to know . . . ?'

'There'd be no such enterprise here in Selburn,' shrugged the tailor. 'Not enough business for them in cattle or mining towns. They'd mostly operate in big cities. Well, state or territorial capitals. The closest would be in Santa Fe. Yes, there is a theatrical costumer there. I know that for sure, but can't recall the name. It escapes me at the moment.'

'How about Arizona?' asked Stretch.

'Phoenix? Tucson maybe?'

'We'd make Santa Fe faster,' countered Larry. 'If we can get passage on a northbound that'll carry our horses.'

'Northbound trains passing through Selburn go all the way to Denver, Colorado,' Onslow told them. 'Santa Fe's a stopover — naturally. It would certainly be faster than travelling horseback.' He eyed Larry curiously. 'Your enquiry is unusual to say the least, but I don't suppose you'd care to explain . . . ?'

'What it gets down to, Mister Onslow, is we got to find a place where eight hombres could buy fake cavalry outfits,' said Larry. 'Can't say no more'n that.'

'Then I have steered you right,' smiled Onslow. 'It *has* to be a theatrical supply house.'

'We're mighty obliged,' declared Larry, as he pocketed the items.

As they led their mounts along Selburn's main stem toward the railroad depot, Stretch demanded to be told, 'How's this gonna help? Hoppin' a train, travellin' all the way up to Santa Fe? Hell, runt, we're losin' time.'

'And Santa Fe's big,' grouched Larry. 'We never were partial to big cities. Too crowded. Every mother's son hustlin'.'

'But we're goin' there anyway?' challenged Stretch.

'Got to,' insisted Larry. 'Here's how I figure it. The Curran deal took a lot of plannin'. They had to do it right, clear the town so nobody'd see 'em grab Zack Dryden's stash. So the boss-thief got this notion they should rig 'emselves like troopers, ride fast into town and spook the citizens with a lot of flim flam about a border raidin' party. And it worked.'

'Because they looked like what they claimed they were,' nodded Stretch.

'So we better hope they picked up the fake outfits in Santa Fe,' said Larry. 'I ain't hopin' for miracles, amigo. I'll settle for a parley with the hombre they dealt with.' He amended that 'Them or just a couple of 'em. We need a name.'

'Which'll likely be as fake as the uniforms,' warned Stretch.

'Maybe so,' agreed Larry. 'But, if we're lucky, if the storeman ain't feeble-minded or half-blind, we might just get a description.'

'You're hopin' for more,' accused Stretch.

'Well, yeah,' Larry admitted.

'Hopin' one of them looters is a Santa Fe man,' said Stretch. 'Long shot, but it could be, huh? He's had time to travel home since they split up.'

At the depot, they learned they could be on their way north 9 a.m. of the morrow. Passage was available on a passenger train to which a box car would be attached. A local horse-breeder was shipping a thoroughbred stallion to a buyer at Albuquerque, so there would be spare stalls for the sorrel and pinto. Larry paid for a one-way trip to Santa Fe, collected their tickets and assured the clerk they would arrive well before departure time.

Located handy to the depot were a stable and a hotel, the Delano. After putting their horses in the care of the hostler, they rented a room at the Delano for their overnight stay and, until suppertime, took their ease in a nearby saloon which happened to be patronized by local sporting men.

They were at the bar, nursing shots of good rye, when the taller Texan observed the longing glance aimed by his partner at a poker table; there was one empty chair.

'We're apt to need every buck of our bankroll,' he chided.

'Might lay out mucho dinero before we nail them fakers, all eight of 'em,' nodded Larry. 'Tell you what. I'll set myself a limit, okay? Fifty. If I lose fifty, I quit the game.'

'Lotsa luck,' shrugged Stretch.

Larry didn't drop $50. At sundown, he came out of that poker party with $180 to add to their bankroll.

They dined at the Delano, turned in early, rose early and, after breakfast, checked out and toted their gear to the stable. Their animals were brought to the depot with time to spare and loaded into the box car, after which they found seats in the second Pullman. On time, the northbound steamed out of Selburn.

Slumped low in his seat, smoking, Stretch wondered aloud about the people of Curran, but three in particular, Belle Fassen and the Drydens.

'Bad times for 'em, so how're they gonna get by? Startin' all over, rebuildin', takes cash. Ain't a saloon for Belle to work in, and what's left of old Zack's store? Not much.'

'Best idea the banker ever had, takin' his safe to the canyon,' drawled Larry. 'The looters would've found some way of bustin' it open, and then all the folks'd be broke as well as homeless. At least they can draw out cash for their needs — all except Zack.'

'Think the banker'll make him a

loan?' asked Stretch.

'I pegged Zack for a mighty independent old hombre,' said Larry. 'Takin' out a loan — he wouldn't like that — but it don't seem he's got a choice.' He was silent a while, brooding. Then, 'We'll get it back from every looter we flush out.'

'Zack's dinero?' prodded Stretch.

'We'll figure whatever cash they're totin's their cut of the loot,' Larry said firmly. 'So we'll take it, keep it for Zack. Mightn't find the whole twenty-five thousand, but maybe we'll collect the hog's share of it for him.'

'Sounds reasonable,' said Stretch.

★ ★ ★

They quit the northbound in Santa Fe at noon of a high temperature day. Saddling their animals, securing Winchesters, packrolls and saddlebags was the easiest way to transport their gear. Mounted and idling their horses along the big town's main thoroughfare, they were at once afflicted with their old hangup, their deep-rooted aversion for centres of civilization so sizeable as to qualify as cities. For them, it had begun long ago. They had been in Chicago through happenstance at the time of the great fire people still remembered. Since that time, they had seen El Paso, Cheyenne, Kansas City, Denver, even San Francisco. Denver. They were reminded of Colorado's capital now.

'Remember Denver?' asked Stretch, grimacing.

'Hard sidewalks,' scowled Larry. 'Electrical street lamps. And them unnatural contraptions folks talk into — with other folks talkin' right back at 'em.'

'Telephones they call 'em,' said Stretch. 'Said it before and I'll say it again. It ain't decent. You want to tell somethin' to a hombre that's someplace else, you can put it on paper, write a letter or telegraph him. I'll go along with that. But palaverin' with a hombre you can't see? Ain't right.'

'Ain't natural,' complained Larry. He nudged his Stetson off his brow and scanned the busiest street they'd seen in years. 'Hell's sakes. How're we gonna find just one place in a town so big?'

He solved the problem by leading his partner leftward. He had spotted Santa Fe's postal telegraph building.

'Every kind of business gets mail, huh?' prodded Stretch.

'And postmasters got to know where to deliver it,' said Larry.

They questioned a clerk who, with a grin, assured them, 'Sure, we know every place of business in the city. We're the mail service after all, what's the name of the place you're looking for?'

'We don't know the name.' Larry tight-reined his impatience. 'But a tailor in Selburn said chances are it's the only such outfit in Santa Fe.'

'If you know what kind of business they're in . . . '

'That much we do know. They rent or sell duds to showfolks.'

'Theatrical supplies, costumes, that kind of stuff.'

'Yep.'

'Well, the tailor at Selburn said it. Only one business of that kind here. Has to be the Orion Company. Caliente Street. That's two blocks up. You turn right and the number's nineteen.' The clerk grinned again after the tall strangers thanked him and started for the entrance. 'You old cowhands thinking of getting into the show business — like Colonel Cody and Bill Hickok did?' They turned to stare at him; he raised a hand placatingly. 'Just joking, gents, just joking.'

'Bite your tongue,' Larry sourly chided.

They managed it, actually found their way to Number 19, Caliente Street, which proved to be a four-storey building. And, according to a man loitering in the street entrance, the Orion company occupied the top floor.

Veteran nomads, they had done a lot of climbing in their time, much of it hazardous. Rocky slants, sometimes almost sheer mountainsides. All this they had survived. But stairs? They didn't mind climbing a flight of stairs. Four flights was something else again. But, when they entered the theatrical costumer's domain, they stifled their resentment and addressed a female assistant with their typical southern courtesy, doffing their Stetsons, not raising their voices.

'The boss?' she smiled. 'That'll be Mister Katz, Mister Stephen Katz. He owns this place. I don't think he's busy right now. May I have your names?'

'He's Valentine, I'm Emerson,' offered Stretch.

'Won't keep you a moment.'

As at Camp Selburn, it was a short wait, and for the same reason. The squatly-built, bright-eyed Stephen Katz was, like Colonel Bostwick, well acquainted with the reputation of the notorious drifters sometimes described

110

by frontier journalists as living legends. Not only did he invite Larry and Stretch into his private office; he insisted they accept cigars, Havanas.

'Edwin Booth and his manager sat in those same chairs,' he enthused as they seated themselves. 'Got to say, gents, I feel as privileged now as on that memorable occasion. It was a surprise visit.'

'Thanks for the cigars and the kind words, Mister Katz, but we ain't special,' frowned Stretch. 'And ain't you never heard you oughtn't believe all you read in the newspapers?'

'Call me Steve,' Katz insisted as he gave them a light.

'If you want, sure,' nodded Stretch. 'So he's Larry and I'm Stretch.'

'My pleasure,' beamed Katz. 'Now — something I can do for you?'

'Uh huh,' grunted Larry. 'How's your memory?'

'It never fails me,' bragged Katz. 'Great memory for figures, costumes, names, faces. I run into a person I haven't seen in ten years, I immediately remember the name.'

'So far, we're doin' just great, huh runt?' grinned Stretch.

'Steve's an old buddy of ours already,' Larry said amiably, digging out the button and fragment of cloth. 'Take a look at these, Steve. Might be from your stock?'

After examining them, Katz was positive.

'My stock for sure. They're from replica cavalry uniforms I keep for various touring companies. Well, reasonable replicas.'

'So here's where they came from?' prodded Larry. Katz nodded emphatically. 'All right now, some time back, maybe not a long time back, you supplied eight cavalry outfits, one for a lieutenant, seven like regular troopers.'

'Straight sale,' offered Katz. 'The buyer paid cash. He supplied the measurements of the other members of his company and I was able to accommodate him.'

Hope surged. Larry worked his cigar to the left side of his mouth and pressed on.

'Just one hombre bought the stuff and took it away?'

'That's right,' said Katz. 'Damn liar called himself Peterson.'

He was studied with increased interest.

'Steve don't like liars,' Stretch remarked.

'We're with you, Steve,' said Larry. 'Hate liars like we hate horse-thieves and rustlers. You want to tell us how come you're so sure this Peterson's a liar?'

'I didn't realize it rightaway, meaning at the time of the purchase,' said Katz. 'He claimed he was wardrobe man and stage manager of a travelling show called Haversham's Players. Well, I'd never heard of the Haversham company, but that didn't matter. There'd be dozens of touring companies I've not yet learned of, so I believed him. But now here's the damnedest coincidence. Life is full of them, right?'

'That's the pure truth, Steve ol' buddy,' agreed Stretch.

'I returned to Santa Fe just yesterday evening,' explained Katz. 'Travelled by buggy, drove myself to Parera and back. It's a town a day and a half's ride southwest of here and my sister Miriam lives there with her husband. They run a nice restaurant, the Silver Spoon. If you're ever in Parera, you should treat yourselves to Miriam's fish pie — melt in your mouths.'

'Fine,' said Larry. 'If we're ever in Parera.'

'You'll probably head for Parera when you've heard me out,' opined Katz. 'You see, this feller who called himself Peterson said the costumes were needed for the Haversham company's next production, a play about the events leading up to the Battle of the Little Big Horn.' He shrugged impatiently. 'Will nobody ever forget that debacle? It was tragic, sure, but a debacle.'

'Don't sidetrack yourself, Steve,'

114

begged Stretch. 'Stay on the trail you're ridin'.'

'Okay,' said Katz. 'During my visit, I accompany my brother-in-law Herman to a saloon for a shot of cheer, an establishment called Barron's Palace. And who do I see running the roulette layout? Same feller. Him for sure. The greasy dark hair with the middle parting, the snub nose, same thick lips and pencil-line mustache. I don't understand this, I remark to Herman. Then I tell him about the feller who called himself Peterson of the Haversham outfit. Can't be the same character, says Herman. That's Rollo Dansley and he's been working here off and on the past couple of years. How do you like that? Now why in blazes would a dealer in a gambling joint pretend he's . . . ?'

'You talk to this Dansley?' demanded Larry.

'I was sore enough to — don't like being lied to,' frowned Katz. 'But Herman said forget it, and Miriam was waiting supper for us — what a supper — so we just finished our drinks and left.'

'Another question, Steve, and it's powerful important,' muttered Larry. 'Take your time answering.'

'Whatever it is, I'll remember,' Katz assured him.

'All right now,' said Larry. 'You think Dansley saw you?'

'Not much chance,' said Katz. 'A lot of sports crowding the roulette table. He was being kept busy, wouldn't have had time to notice me.' He grinned eagerly. 'Any more questions? Come on, try me. I'll back my memory against an elephant's.'

'Uses a lot of pomade,' said Larry. 'Parts his hair in the middle, a thick-lipped jasper with one of them thin mustaches and a snub nose. What else can you recollect about him?'

'Dresses flashy, a real dude,' Katz recalled. He half-closed his eyes. 'Let me think now. Anything else? Well, certainly. Ring on his left pinky. Fake diamond. *Has* to be a fake. If he owned a genuine diamond that size, he wouldn't be tending a game of chance in a cowtown saloon, would he?'

'What about his build?' asked Larry.

'Getting paunchy,' said Katz.

'How tall?' prodded Stretch.

Katz promptly rose from his chair.

'This tall. We were side by side while I was showing him the uniforms and I clearly remember we were shoulder to shoulder, dead level. That'd make him five feet and nine inches.' He sank into his chair as the trouble-shooters rose from theirs. 'I'll bet there's quite a story behind all this, but I shouldn't ask *you* any questions?'

'What you don't know can't harm you none, friend,' said Stretch.

'We never asked,' stressed Larry. 'Okay?'

'Okay,' said Katz.

'And we owe you, Steve,' declared Larry, as they shook hands. 'Even if we never see you again, you're a buddy of ours.'

'That makes me real proud,' grinned Katz.

'Good trail southwest to Parera, huh?' Larry asked as they retreated to the office door. 'I mean, if you take a buggy ride regular.'

'Oh, sure,' nodded Katz. 'Straight most of the way. It's a stage route. Been a pleasure talking to you boys.'

'And you've been a big help,' said Stretch. 'Muchas gracias, amigo.' When they had descended the four flights and were untying their horses, he said vehemently, 'Dansley has to be one of 'em.'

'Bet your saddle,' growled Larry.

'We're headin' for Parera rightaway,' guessed Stretch.

'Right after we pick up a few supplies,' said Larry. 'Chow, more tobacco, couple bottles of rye.'

The trail southwest was as Katz had described it. Toward late afternoon, they rode off it to make for a grove and night-camp there. The taller Texan was as patient as ever; he needed to be, because Larry waited until they had finished supper and were lingering over tin cups of coffee spiked with whiskey before laying out his plan. Stretch interrupted just as he began talking, and only to predict, 'This'll be some trick we've pulled before.'

'If it's worked before . . . ' said Larry.

'Yeah, we could score again,' nodded Stretch. 'Go ahead.'

'Maybe Dansley's the only one of the eight in Parera,' said Larry. 'Or, for all we know, there might be more of 'em there. So, if we light a fire under Dansley, maybe we smoke out the others. That's how we'll handle it. Then we'll rent a hotel-room and, like you said, an old trick. And why not? I should pick my brains figurin' a new angle?'

'Same old deal.' Stretch grinned reminiscently. 'Just hole up and wait for 'em to make the next move.'

'And don't let's forget,' Larry emphasized. 'If we have to shoot our way out of a ruckus, we help ourselves to his bank-roll, any hombre we drop.'

'Need to get that done muy pronto,' decided Stretch. 'It could happen late, and gunshots rouse badge-toters damn quick.'

'Best call it a day,' urged Larry, draining his cup. 'When we hit Parera, we're gonna have to be bright-eyed, bushy-tailed and ready for anything any sonofabitch throws at us.'

* * *

Parera looked to be another Curran, another New Mexico cattletown, but bigger, as big as Selburn, when the tall riders sighted it 4.30 p.m. of the following day. They approached unhurriedly and, as they entered the main street, Larry scanned the buildings south of the thoroughfare. Stretch kept his eyes on the other side, waiting to spot a livery stable.

'See it?' he asked, when they had

120

travelled three blocks.

'Uh huh,' grunted Larry. 'Barron's Palace.'

'Bueno.' Stretch gestured. 'Barn over here.'

'So,' said Larry. 'We check our critters in, then pay a call.'

They left their animals with a stablehand, informing him they would be back for their gear later. Stretch remarked, as they emerged from the barn, he had also noted the location of the Silver Spoon Cafe.

'Ought to have quite an appetite after we're through fazin' Mister Rollo Dansley.'

'Right. We'll eat — after we've done that.'

It was done quietly and with relentless cunning. Larry was thinking of Todd Melrose, beloved nephew of Zack and Carrie Dryden, when they ambled into the big saloon and worked their way across to the long bar. Todd Melrose, undoubtedly marked for interrogation by a stranger who had hung around

Curran long enough to note that the town's only merchant never banked his takings, descended upon some time after he left Curran, held prisoner, suffering intense pain until, when he could take no more, he revealed his uncle's hiding place — and signed his own death warrant. Such were Larry's dark thoughts as, with his partner, he breasted the bar and signalled the dispenser of cheer.

They drank passable whiskey, rolled and lit quirleys and covertly surveyed the early evening customers and the staff, particularly the latter. Their gaze drifted from the housemen supervizing the dice, faro and monte tables to the paunchy dude working the roulette layout.

'That's him for sure,' Stretch drawled from the side of his mouth.

'Dansley,' nodded Larry. 'Slick-haired and snub-snooted, thick-lipped mouth and a fake diamond on his left pinky. He's the one called himself Peterson in Santa Fe.'

'You about ready to wipe that smile off his kisser?' asked Stretch.

'About ready,' said Larry.

They drained their glasses and took their time drifting across to the roulette table.

'Number Twenty,' Dansley announced as the white ball stopped clattering and settled into that little hollow. 'The house wins, gents.'

His half-dozen clients gave up in chagrin and moved on to other games of chance, leaving him to be confronted by two tall, grim-faced strangers.

'Place your bets, boys.' He went into his spiel. 'Choose a number, cross your fingers, the wheel turns and where the ball drops nobody knows till . . . '

'That dude outfit,' said Larry, watching his eyes, 'looks just right on you — better'n a fake cavalry uniform.'

The eyes flickered, just as he expected.

'Is that remark supposed to make sense?' challenged Dansley.

'I reckon so,' said Larry. 'Dansley's the name, right?'

'Who wants to know?' demanded Dansley.

'We know anyway,' drawled Stretch. 'My buddy's Lawrence. I'm Woodville — and you're Dansley.'

'But you called yourself Peterson in Santa Fe,' said Larry. ''Less you got a twin brother, you're the jasper picked up eight army outfits from the Orion store in Santa Fe a little while back.'

'I don't know a damn thing about . . .' began Dansley.

'Then a town called Curran got spooked by eight bastards rigged like soldiers,' growled Larry. 'Wasn't enough they got what they came for after the townfolk cut and run. They had to start fires.'

'This is all news to me,' protested Dansley. 'Curran you say? I never heard of it.'

'Fired the calaboose too,' Stretch said bitterly. 'We know, on account of we were locked in there.'

'Couldn't get out,' scowled Larry, watching sweat bead on Dansley's

124

brow. 'Hollered — begged to be turned loose. One of them fake soldiers heard us. Know what he did? Just laughed. Said stay and fry.'

'This is obviously a case of mistaken identity,' blustered Dansley. 'Nothing you're saying means anything to me.'

'Means *plenty* — and you know it,' Larry retorted. 'Now you can get back to your chores. But we'll talk again, Dansley. Count on it.'

With no show of haste, the Texans turned and departed. But, once outside the building, they turned left and hustled into the side alley. An open window a little way along offered a clear view of the interior. They saw a red-faced Dansley mop his face with a silk handkerchief and high sign a hefty, unshaven local propping up the bar, who promptly joined him. Facial expressions fascinated the watchers for a few moments. Dansley was speaking urgently, the hefty man registering astonishment. Though he couldn't eavesdrop from this distance,

Larry was certain the hefty man was receiving instructions. He hurried out.

The trouble-shooters returned to the alleymouth, peeked around the corner and spotted Dansley's friend hurrying uptown.

'Gettin' help?' suggested Stretch.

'That'd be my guess,' said Larry. 'We'll give 'em a minute or two, then find us a hotel and get set up. No hurry.'

Later, when they reappeared on the street, dawdling to the livery stable, they were sure they were under observation; their short hairs told them so. They collected their gear and toted it along the north sidewalk till they reached a hotel, the Jeffers House. Resisting the impulse to glance over their shoulders, they entered the lobby to be greeted by the desk-clerk.

'Rear room,' ordered Larry, dropping money on the desk. 'Got an upstairs double?'

'Sure,' said the clerk. 'Two soft beds, nice clean sheets. Number Thirteen

— unless you gents're superstitious?'

'Sometimes,' shrugged Larry. 'But tonight we're feelin' lucky.' After he and Stretch had inscribed the names Lawrence and Woodville, he accepted the key. 'We'll just stash our stuff and go eat. Be back later.'

They climbed the stairs, followed the corridor to the rear and unlocked the door numbered 13. Stretch scratched a match to life and got the lamp working, while Larry closed the door. They dumped their gear, after which Larry crossed to the window to open it and raise the shade.

'Looks okay?' asked Stretch.

'Couldn't be better.' Larry checked the area outside, withdrew his head and reported. 'Gallery out there. Bound to be firestairs. That's good. I don't want for 'em to have too much trouble reachin' us.'

'Now we eat?'

'Sure. Let's find out if sister Miriam's fish pie's as elegant as brother Steve claims.'

At the cafe, they dined on Miriam's fish pie and a fine dessert, but decided against presenting themselves as friends of the management. They were preoccupied anyway, their appetites unaffected, but Rollo Dansley on their minds, his reaction to Larry's scare tactics.

Near the end of their supper, Stretch offered the hunch the hefty local confided in by Dansley could be another of the eight.

'Well, sure, it figures,' Larry agreed. 'When the chips're down and a skunk starts frettin', he'll always turn to his own kind.'

'Things could get kind of hectic,' predicted Stretch. 'But we better not forget we made old Zack a promise. We have to take a live one and spook some answers out of him.'

'Promised we'd do our damnedest,' muttered Larry. 'That's the most you and me can promise — any time.'

On their way back to the hotel, he observed, without seeming too,

128

the hefty man watching from the opposite sidewalk, and not alone now. His companion was just as bulky, but was not Dansley.

When they returned to Room 13, the taller Texan rolled and lit a cigarette, glanced about and remarked, 'I guess it ain't too early.'

'Might's well make a start,' shrugged Larry.

And they began their preparations while, in the poky office fronting the town jail, the local law-men took their ease.

5

Hot Pursuit

OVERWEIGHT Tom McGinn and his one aide, the just as overweight Luke Steggle, were content with their lot, complacent in fact. Despite its size and the presence of several cattle spreads in this general area, Parera had become an orderly town. A low crime rate meant McGinn and Steggle spent much time in idleness, their favorite condition. And the marshal's office with its eight-cell calaboose was their favorite habitat. Rent rooms in a hotel, live at a boarding house? Not for them. Sleeping on the sagging office couch or a cell bunk, they mutually agreed, was a sensible economy. Well, it made no dent in their monthly stipend as keepers of the peace of Parera.

'We got it made, Luke,' yawned moon-faced McGinn, slumped low in his swivel chair with his boot-heels resting on the edge of his untidy desk. 'No way I'd ever quit this job.'

'Beats the hell out of totin' a badge in Albuquerque or Alamogordo, huh?' drawled jowly Steggle. 'Lively towns, wild towns, you can have 'em for mine. Gimme Parera any time.'

'Progress, that's what keeps us lazy, and I wouldn't have it any other way,' McGinn said smugly. 'Progress and civilization — like we got right here in Parera. Had to happen. Cowhands don't all stay ornery their whole lives. They get wed, a lot of 'em. They settle down and sire young 'uns, so they got responsibilities, so no more hellin' around, no more brannigans in saloons. They save their pay now. It's only the regular sportin' men and the well-heeled towners that can afford to gamble.'

'Ain't been a badman hit this town in a month of Sundees,' said Steggle.

'That suits me fine.'

They traded contented grins, the marshal comfortable in his chair, his deputy horizontal on the couch.

'Suits me too,' declared McGinn.

'As for Herbie Jence, I ain't frettin' about what he said,' mumbled Steggle. 'Durn fool don't see so good anyway. Needs eye-glasses. Couldn't've saw who he claims he saw.'

'Herbie claimed he saw Bat Masterson playin' poker at the High Spade Saloon a couple months ago,' McGinn recalled. 'Turned out it wasn't him at all. Just a drygoods drummer from Colorado.'

'Sure.' Steggle yawned unconcernedly. 'So it couldn't be them he saw.'

Conversation between marshal and deputy was usually conducted at snail's pace. A full three and a half minutes passed before McGinn got around to enquiring, 'Who'd Herbie say he saw?'

Another long pause.

'Valentine and Emerson, them Texas Trouble-Shooters,' said Steggle. 'Before sundown. Ridin' in slow.'

McGinn winced.

'Just as well it was Herbie,' he said with great relief. 'He's bound to be wrong. If some other feller claimed he saw 'em, I'd worry some. They're trouble, them drifters.'

'I've heard it said it ain't them that's dangerous,' offered Steggle. 'It's the strife that follows 'em every place they show up. *That's* what's dangerous.'

'If we're ever that unlucky, meanin' if Valentine and his sidekick ever show up here, there's only one smart way we should deal with 'em,' insisted McGinn. 'I've heard tell of other lawmen that cussed 'em out or tried to lean heavy on 'em, and some that even arrested 'em. Big mistake, Luke. Terrible mistake. Them poor jaspers ended up nervous wrecks. Them trouble-shooters gave 'em hell. Well, by dad, *we* ain't makin' that mistake.'

'What's the only smart way to deal with 'em?' frowned Steggle.

'Gentle,' decided McGinn. 'Polite.

Plumb friendly. No harsh words, no hassle. Where's the sense to makin' 'em mad at us? Do we need that kind of tribulation?'

'Hell, no,' Steggle said warmly. 'I don't want them hell-raisers tribulatin' me. No, sir. Not so you'd notice.'

'I've seen pictures of 'em,' confided McGinn, grimacing uneasily. 'They're taller'n tall and tougher'n tough.'

They relaxed, ridding their minds of fears of notorious nomads, clamorous gunfights, pitched saloon brawls so violent as to cause extensive damage to property, and other such upheaval.

'You want to bunk on the couch tonight?' asked Steggle.

'That's where I slept last night,' said McGinn. 'Fair's fair. You stay where you're at. Cell bunk'll do me fine.'

In Room 13 of the Jeffers House, the Texans were as ready as they would ever be. Their lamp still burned. The window was locked and the shade drawn. Bootless and hatless, they stood arms akimbo and surveyed their come-and-get-us trap.

The night being warm, few Parera citizens would use a blanket; a sheet was as much covering as any sleeper could tolerate. The drifters had used their blankets, but for another purpose, bunching them around spare pillows, cushions, anything they could find in this room for the sake of making the beds appear occupied. Sheets were drawn up to cover these improvised dummies. From a hook in the wall beside the locked door their shellbelts dangled. Larry had rammed his Colt into the back of his Levis. Stretch had followed his example with one of his. His second Colt was still holstered, the butt protruding. As seen from the window, no lamplight, maybe moonlight, it would appear they had hung all their sidearms on that hook above their boots, their Stetsons resting atop the boots.

'Looks okay,' decided Stretch.

'It'll do,' nodded Larry. 'Now we

hide out ourselves, but careful. I don't crave to catch no crossfire.'

'Me neither,' Stretch assured him. 'So where do we stake out?'

'Kill the lamp, open the window and raise the shade,' urged Larry. 'We need to know how much they can see from the gallery.'

Stretch obeyed. They waited to get their eyes accustomed to the half-dark. Because of his formidable height, Stretch moved to the side wall, spread his long arms, took hold of the wardrobe and moved it forward. He could fit into the space now separating the back of it from the wall.

'This'll do me,' he announced.

'Uh huh,' grunted Larry, his eyes busy. The corner right of the washstand was in complete darkness. He sidled over there and hunkered. 'Take a look from over by the window. Tell me if you can see me.'

His partner checked and assured him that was as good a hiding place as any.

'So now we wait it out?'

'Now we wait it out,' muttered Larry.

From now until the anticipated intrusion, conversation would be pointless. It wasn't a new situation for them. They would know what to do when the time came.

It began a few minutes after 1 a.m. Thanks to their sensitive hearing, they were well warned; the footsteps somewhere down below were almost inaudible. A plank creaked, indicating the firestairs were being climbed. Larry figured more than one man. Two, maybe three. Then they were outside the open window and both Texans heard the quietly voiced command and recognized the voice.

'Get it done fast!'

Dansley. Standing guard out there on the gallery while, one by one, his two cohorts climbed into the room. For a brief moment, they stood quiet, staring at the beds. One inched toward the bed nearest the window, his companion making for the other. Larry watched with gun in hand and fury in his heart and Stretch thrust head and gunhand out from behind the wardrobe as knives were drawn and raised. Hard and fast, the would-be killers thrust and jabbed and hacked — until one of them loosed a gasp. Larry rose to his full height, growled his challenge and promptly dropped to one knee.

'Wrong place.'

'That ain't where we are,' announced Stretch.

They heard the clatter of the dropped knives. Both marauders emptied holsters and fired, the reports sounding as thunder. Just before the first shot, just before he fired in retaliation, Larry heard the third man retreating in frantic haste. Stretch's gun roared. Five shots were fired, three by the marauders, one apiece by the Texans, and the sounds next heard weren't gunshots. The thud was Larry's victim hitting the floor. The lesser sound was the second man flopping crosswise on a bed.

'Light the lamp,' said Larry. 'We got somethin' to do before the local law pounds on our door.'

Stretch made for the lamp, scratching a match en route. Yellow light filled the room again, revealing the man sprawled across a bed and the one huddled on the floor. They didn't move; death had been instantaneous.

Quickly, the drifters checked pockets. Stretch emptied a wallet while Larry tugged a wad of bills from a back pocket. He was thrusting the banknotes inside his shirt when the pounding began, also the chorus of shocked exclamations and shouted questions in the corridor. Stretch chose to answer only one question — the loudest.

'What's happening in there? Open this door! Damn it, this is *my hotel*! I'm Waldo Jeffers!'

'Don't get your nightshirt in a knot, Mister Jeffers,' called Stretch, moving to the door. 'Trouble's all over. I'm openin' up now.'

'If there's women out there, they

better not come in,' warned Larry.

Stretch unlocked and opened the door to admit the hotel-keeper, a short man, hair tousled, a bathrobe covering his sleeping attire. Jeffers gawked at the bodies and recoiled in shock.

'Anybody sent for the sheriff?' asked Stretch.

'The m-m-marshal you m-mean,' faltered Jeffers. 'Marshal McGinn'll be here soon enough. His office isn't that far away and — all that shooting would wake the dead!'

By the time McGinn arrived, Jeffers had cleared the corridor of bug-eyed busybodies and the Texans had donned boots and hats and were strapping on their gunbelts. Though he had donned only his boots — he owned no bathrobe nor slippers — the official status of this moon-faced local was at once apparent to the strangers; he had attached his badge to the front of his nightshirt before venturing forth, a reflex action.

'What in blue blazes . . . ?' he began. 'Holy Moses! You're them

Texans — the trouble-shooters!'

He stared aghast, he and Jeffers, at the bodies, the blood, the dropped knives and six-guns, the bullet-pitted walls.

'Look — uh — I know this looks bad,' soothed Stretch, who tended to understate sometimes. 'But don't get no wrong ideas about us, Marshal suh.'

'Like you can see, we were expectin' trouble,' Larry pointed out. 'So we made it look like we were sleepin' and, when these sonsabitches climbed in and put their knives into what they thought was us . . . '

'We called 'em on it and they got to shootin',' said Stretch. 'Had to defend ourselves, didn't we?'

'You got to admit that's reasonable,' suggested Larry.

Jeffers was wringing his hands, but the marshal rallying and not relishing an argument with two hard-boiled survivors.

'Reasonable, yeah.' He nodded

eagerly. 'I got no quarrel with you gents.'

Now Steggle came blundering in, half-dressed, toting a shot-gun and in an advanced state of agitation.

'What the hell's happenin' to this town?' he cried. 'I near got stomped by that dude's horse! He rid outa town like a hunnerd Injuns was after his scalp!'

'*What dude?*' demanded Larry.

The deputy tried not to cringe.

'Dansley — him that runs the roulette set-up at . . . '

'Whichaway'd he head?' growled Larry.

'Straight for the trail,' mumbled Steggle. 'He'll be headed southwest.' His gaze switched to the dead men. 'Holy cow! Bud Rettig and Joe Woodward!'

'Local hard cases of low account,' McGinn informed the Texans. 'We've had 'em — uh — under suspicion for quite a time. They ain't gonna be missed.'

'You said you got no quarrel with us,' Larry reminded him. 'We've told you how this happened so, if you got no more questions, we got unfinished business with that dude.'

'Had to be like we said,' drawled Stretch. 'You won't find no bullet-holes in their backs.'

'Self-defence — that's clear enough,' McGinn readily agreed.

'What about the bullet-holes in my walls?' wailed Jeffers.

But the lawmen weren't listening nor making any attempt to delay the trouble-shooters, who hastily gathered up their gear. Moments later they were at the livery stable, readying their mounts, securing saddlebags, packrolls and rifles. The stablehand came awake and was tossed a coin, after which they hustled their animals into the moonlight, swung astride and heeled them to a run.

Out of Parera and following the southwest trail, Larry insisted they ease their pace.

'How far's that skunk gonna lead us d'you suppose?' asked Stretch. 'Runt, that was him outside on the gallery, nothin' surer.'

'Somethin' else is just as sure,' declared Larry. 'The two we had to gun down were in Curran recent. Quite a passel of dinero we took from 'em, and you can bet your butt it came from Zack's cashbox.'

'So,' said Stretch. 'Two down, six to go. And maybe the dude'll lead us to more of 'em?'

'That's what I'm countin' on,' nodded Larry. 'And that's why we're gonna give him space. Can't afford for him to spot us taggin' him. He might try to draw us elsewhere.'

'Yeah, well, we ain't doin' nothin' we ain't done before,' remarked Stretch. 'Bird-dog a rider runnin' scared, hang back so he don't know we're on his trail.'

An hour later, with the moonlight holding, they paused to spell their animals. Stretch stared ahead, then

144

sprawled to press an ear to the ground.

'Still movin',' guessed Larry.

'Sure is,' said Stretch, getting to his feet. 'And I'm tellin' you, even if he's straddlin' a high-class mount, a thoroughbred, it'll be plumb draggin' its hooves time he gets to where he's headed. He's *really* runnin' scared, runt.'

'Got plenty to be scared of,' Larry said grimly. 'It didn't work out like he planned. He knew we'd set a trap soon as the guns started poppin'.'

He raised his eyes to the sky. 'Got a feelin' in my bones. Be sun-up by the time he quits this trail — *if* he quits it. And we'll cut his sign.'

'He could be headed for another town?'

'Your guess is as good as mine.'

'Well, we got one thing goin' for us.'

'Damn right. When the chips're down, scum like him run for help — and I don't mean a helper with a tin star. Birds of a feather, you know?'

'Yup, we could get lucky again. We catch up with Dansley, we catch up with another of them fake horse soldiers.'

Having spelled their horses, they took turns to swig from a bottle. When they moved on, they were chewing jerky; if they couldn't sleep, they could at least keep up their strength.

At sunrise, with Parera far behind them, they easily read tracks of a hard-ridden horse for another mile of the trail. They found, too, the point at which their quarry had wheeled his mount left to detour across the prairie east. The hoof-prints told them Dansley was pushing on desperately, pushing a winded animal to the limits of its endurance.

'Here's where he *had* to slow down,' Stretch observed, as they reined up for a closer look.

Larry nodded agreement and stared farther east, glimpsing cattle. He now got around to drawing his Colt, ejecting a spent shell and reloading; Stretch did likewise. Was their quarry making for a ranch headquarters? It seemed so.

'Ride wary from here on,' muttered Larry.

Travelling grazeland now, they approached a brushy rise, keeping its bulk between them and whatever lay beyond. The near slope was gentle, not too steep for their horses, but they took them only three-quarter way to the summit, dismounted and ground-reined them. Larry dug out his field-glasses and, side by side, they climbed up top and bellied down.

In the distance, well east of a sizeable herd of prime stock, they could see the ranch-house, corrals and other buildings, also a slow-moving rider. Propping his elbows, Larry adjusted the glasses to bring the horseman into close focus.

'Dansley,' he said.

'As if you hadn't guessed,' said Stretch. 'So how about this? If a cattle spread's where he plans on holin' up, we could be tanglin' with a rogue-rancher and a whole bunkhouse full of cowwaddies as crooked as Dansley.'

'Let's wait and see,' frowned Larry, still following the rider's movements.

He saw much that intrigued him, reporting each detail to his partner, Dansley dismounting, the chuck-boss emerging from the cook-shack to speak with the visitor a moment, then trudging to a bunkhouse. A few minutes later, the chuck-boss reappeared with three men following. He returned to the cook-shack. The three moved to where Dansley waited.

'Powwow?' prodded Stretch.

'He's no stranger to 'em,' opined Larry. 'Uh huh. Powwow. But not there. One of 'em's takin' Dansley's weary critter to a barn. The other two're fetchin' saddles now, headin' for a horse corral.'

'Seems like we'll be ridin' again pretty soon,' said Stretch.

Larry watched in silence till the four were mounted, Dansley astride a fresh animal. When the riders moved out, he grinned wryly and lowered his glasses.

'We won't need to mount up again,' he opined. 'Not if they're headed for . . .'

'Hey, they're headed toward *us*,' growled Stretch.

'Not *right* toward us,' countered Larry. 'Take a look at what's away right of us — and what's in between us and it.'

'Timber,' Stretch noted. 'Could be a clearin' inside of that copse. They want to keep everything private.' He studied the terrain between their vantage-point and the stand of trees — thick-grassed and showing many a brush-clump. 'Sure, I catch your drift. If they don't ride out of the timber after they're into it, we head thataway on our feet. Plenty brush to screen us. We get close enough for a little spyin', we could learn a thing or two.'

Further discussion would have been superfluous. They descended to their horses, unfastened their spurs and, from the base of the rise, watched the four riders approach and enter the copse. It didn't take long for them to realize they were staying in there, so now they headed in that direction, bent low and hugging every piece of cover they could find, drawing ever closer to the near edge of the trees.

Muffled voices reached them, a warning they should drop to all fours. Through the trees they crawled, taking pains to move clear of dry twigs that would surely snap under a knee or an elbow and betray their presence. The nicker of a horse and a growled comment guided them to the clearing, the four animals tied left of it, the men hunkered in a circle. Surveying the group from behind thick trunks, the eavesdroppers reflected Dansley was in rough company right now, three hard-eyed men in range clothes, each packing a tied-down, low-holstered Colt. Dansley's coat was open, so they would remember he too was armed; they glimpsed the harness of an armpit holster.

Larry got the impression Dansley had finished reporting the fate suffered by two cronies in a Parera hotel-room. The other men were giving vent to profanity. One spat in disgust and muttered, 'Bud and Joe — hell. And you figured it'd be easy. But now they're grave-bait.'

'You always were a gutless tinhorn and slow-brained, Dansley,' another man accused.

'Jard, I don't have to take that from you,' scowled Dansley.

'Think, damn you!' snarled Jard. 'It never crossed your mind they'd tag you out of Parera — and you'd lead 'em to us?'

'Impossible.' Dansley spoke vehemently. 'That possibility did cross my mind so, all the way here, I kept checking my back trail. I'm sure I wasn't followed.'

'Who the hell are they anyway?' wondered the leanest of his companions. 'You told us how they braced you in

Parera. How'd they know what they were talkin' about?'

'Look, Slim, I've asked myself those questions a hundred times since quitting Parera,' muttered Dansley. 'All I got was their names — Lawrence and Woodville. How they connected me with the costumes is beyond my comprehension. Got rid of the stuff, didn't we? Followed Anson's plan all the way, burned everything before we divided the take and went our separate ways? I don't understand what could've gone wrong.'

'I'd've sworn Anse Miller thought of everything,' said the man with the beak-like nose and heavy-lidded eyes.

'I too, Eddie,' nodded Dansley. 'He got the information and, as far as I could understand, he used it right. The Curran deal was a pushover.'

'With Miller and Watling settlin' for them damn beads,' muttered Eddie. 'The cash for us, the jewellery for them. And now I'm thinkin' their share's worth a whole lot more'n what we took outa that tin box.'

'I've had the same idea,' said Dansley.

'Hey, I bet you lost yours,' jeered Slim.

'Don't rub it in,' said Dansley, wincing.

'You're a fool,' chided Jard. 'You should stick to runnin' a roulette layout and stay far clear of five card stud. Comes to poker, you ain't got what it takes. You lose your shirt every time.'

'We're some smarter'n you, tinhorn,' taunted Jard, patting his hip pocket. 'We still got ours.'

'You shouldn't've told him, Jard,' leered Slim. 'Now he'll put the arm on us for a handout.'

'Forty-three dollars is all I have left,' said Dansley. 'But I didn't ride down from Parera to beg for cash. I say we should get clear out of New Mexico.'

'Feel safer with us, huh?' challenged Eddie.

'Those tall jaspers're gun-fast and full of tricks,' said Dansley. 'I admit

I don't want to end up as dead as Bud and Joe. And, yes, there's safety in numbers. We'll get no help from Anson or Hal. They're too far away now. So we should stick together.

'Why should *we* run?' countered Jard. 'Rafter K's where we ought to stay. Far as the boss knows, we're just three of his hired hands. When we're good and ready to quit, we'll quit with better'n three thousand in our pockets.'

'I figure we can afford to bide our time,' said Eddie.

'Where would you run to anyway?' Jard challenged Dansley.

''Frisco,' said Dansley, licking his lips. 'I think Anson will be reasonable when I walk in on him. After all, he handed me the chore of organizing those uniforms. It didn't seem a risky chore at the time, but now I know different, don't I? So it ought to be worth a little extra.'

'I don't reckon Anse'd take kindly to that,' warned Jard. 'He said we should stay clear of him and Hal, and a deal's a deal.'

'Stay out of 'Frisco,' Slim coldly advised. 'Suit yourself where you run to, tinhorn, long as it ain't 'Frisco. As for us, we'll quit when we're good and ready.

'Come on now, boys . . . ' began Dansley.

'He's gonna beg,' predicted Jard. He laughed and both Texans felt their gorges rise and their scalps crawl. They had heard that distinctive, gurgling laugh before. 'Hey, this'll be funny!'

'Go on, tinhorn,' sneered Eddie. 'Make your pitch. We want to hear you beg. It won't help you any, but we could use a laugh.'

'Quitting this territory is the logical thing for us to do,' insisted Dansley. 'Safety in numbers I said.'

'And *I* said,' Slim reminded him, '*we* ain't quittin' till we're good and ready.'

'*Nobody's* quittin',' growled Larry, stepping out into clear view with Stretch following. They stood tall while the four struggled upright, gaping at them.

'Easy now — soldier-boys. Keep them paws . . .'

'Far clear of your hardware,' warned Stretch.

'It's them!' gasped Dansley.

'You damn jackass, Dansley!' raged Slim. 'You led 'em to us!'

'Hell . . . !' breathed Eddie.

'Next stop for four fake soldier-boys — the nearest sheriff's office,' announced Larry. 'And, if you're thinkin' rash, thinkin' you can outfight us, you better do some listenin'.'

'Which might change your minds,' muttered Stretch.

'We're the hombres you heard hollerin' when you set the Curran jail afire,' declared Larry, his narrowed eyes fastening on Jard. 'Ain't forgotten us, have you? You laughed. Stay and fry, you said.'

'So,' drawled Stretch. 'Do we owe you skunks a break?'

'Don't . . .'

Larry began another warning, but didn't finish it. They weren't listening. Jard, Slim and Eddie were drawing and Dansley's right hand was darting under his coat. It was that time again, time for the trouble-shooters to resort to their dazzling gun-speed, Larry drawing, cocking and firing all in one flash of movement, Stretch emptying his holsters faster than the eye could follow.

Jard's Colt was levelled when Larry's first bullet hit him dead centre and drove him to the ground. Stretch's matched .45s boomed in unison and, while Slim died on his feet, Dansley's derby was torn away by the slug from Stretch's lefthand gun; he reeled drunkenly with his head bloody and his .38 Smith & Wesson discharging into the ground, and then Eddie's gun roared. Larry flinched to the hot wind of the bullet fanning his right ear and promptly returned fire and, with a ragged groan, Eddie collapsed and writhed.

He had stopped writhing when Stretch moved to him to rid him of his weapon. Larry extricated another Colt from a dead hand, tossed it aside, then moved to the huddled and unconscious Dansley.

'Three done for,' said Stretch. 'Believe it.'

'You're no liar, beanpole,' said Larry, on his knees now, studying Dansley's wound. 'Just three. Not all four of 'em. This time, old Zack gets his wish. We took us a live one.'

'The dude,' Stretch said in disgust.

'Your slug tore his scalp right where he parts his greasy hair,' muttered Larry. 'When he rouses, he'll have a headache like he'd never believe, and he'll give us some answers.' As he moved to one of the horses to unhitch a canteen, he reminded Stretch. 'They bragged they were packin' three thousand a piece. No use to 'em now, but Zack sure needs it.'

Stretch took the hint and made fast work of relieving their victims of money not paid them for tending cattle. He shoved the cash inside his shirt and moved across to join his partner. With Dansley's own handkerchief, moistened from a canteen, Larry swabbed blood from the face and the pomaded head.

'What kind of fool'd crave such a little bitty mustache?' wondered the taller Texan. 'Will you look at that thing? I ask you, runt, can you see yourself shavin' your top lip so slow and careful — to show a line of whiskers scarce a half-inch wide?'

'*That'll* be the day,' growled Larry.

'How about his roll?' asked Stretch.

'You heard what he told his companeros, and I believe it,' said Larry. 'He's down to a lousy forty-three bucks and he's alive. I don't want to be slowed down by him wailin' we robbed him when we turn him over to the law.'

'He comin' round?'

'Not yet, but he's breathin' steady.'

'So now what? We tie these stiffs on their horses and . . . ?'

'Might's well get on with it,' said Larry.

Before beginning that chore, they built and lit cigarettes. They were replacing spent shells, reloading their Colts, when they heard the hoofbeats. Riders were approaching.

6

Legal Expenses

THE taller drifter hooked thumbs in his buscadero shellbelt and asked,

'Who? You want to make a guess?'

'No,' said Larry. 'Sounds like they're comin' on fast, but they're still a ways off. How about you take a look?'

'They heard the shootin',' Stretch opined as he began quitting the clearing. 'You could make book on that.'

Dansley groaned and stirred, but with his eyes still closed. Larry waited. He was calm, not yet feeling elation, though in no doubt five of the predators of Curran had paid the supreme penalty for their treachery. Right now, the riders alerted by the din of this shootout were his big concern. If they became aggressive, there could be more trouble here.

Stretch returned.

'Three,' he reported. 'I let 'em see me, waved to 'em friendly, so maybe they won't come chargin' in here with their hoglegs pointed at us.'

'What d'you make of 'em?' demanded Larry.

'One's a young'un — plenty young I think,' drawled Stretch. 'Other two're older. They ain't townmen. Cattlemen from the looks of 'em.'

'Comin' from the ranch?' frowned Larry. Stretch nodded. 'Well, this piece of timber's likely on some hombre's home range, so he's got a right to get curious.'

They heard the horsemen ease their mounts to a walk as they neared the copse. Side by side they stood, faces devoid of expression. That was how the two ageing cattlemen and their younger companion saw them as they warily entered the clearing.

Larry made a quick study. The older

two were of an age, nudging fifty, heavyset, their weather-beaten faces adorned by full mustaches. He pegged the young one for nineteen, but a fast-maturing nineteen, already wearing the look of a regular ranch-hand. His expression, as his gaze fell on the dead men, was solemn. The older men were grim-faced. After an intent scrutiny of the trouble-shooters' victims, one of them growled, 'You're on my land. Kelsey's my name, Burch Kelsey. Rafter K's my brand. I recognize three of these dead men as . . . '

'The hombre you don't recognize, the dude, is a thief we tailed from Parera,' Larry interrupted.

'And he'll live to have his day in court, Mister Kelsey,' said Stretch.

'Three of 'em are — were — on my payroll,' declared Kelsey. He identified his companions. 'This is my boy Clem and my foreman, Holly Freestone. And now I figure it's up to you to name yourselves and tell me what happened here.'

'I'm Valentine, my partner's Emerson and the live one's Rollo Dansley,' offered Larry. 'Like I said, we tagged him out of Parera and all the way to your spread.'

'And he's a lowdown sonofabitch thief,' Stretch said flatly.

'In Parera, two of Dansley's buddies tried to kill us,' continued Larry, as Freestone dismounted for a closer inspection of the losers. 'Couldn't let 'em do that, could we? The Parera undertaker's planted 'em by now. That spooked Dansley, so he cut and run with us bird-doggin' him. From over thataway, atop a little rise, we saw him ride clear to your place. Then him and these hombres came here for a private parley and, before we braced 'em, we did some listenin', so I can guarantee you ain't lost three fair-thinkin' honest hands.'

For his boss's benefit, the ramrod named the losers.

'Eddie Goff, Jard Horner and Slim Ringle.' He added. 'They were doin' it again, Burch, maybe quittin' the spread without as much as a beg pardon, just like last time.'

'I know what you're thinking, Holly,' scowled Kelsey. 'I should've fired 'em when they came back — after being gone who knows where for a week or more.'

His son remarked, 'You *would've* fired 'em, if we weren't so short-handed.'

'Said you braced 'em?' challenged Kelsey.

'They had their chance to surrender,' Larry assured him. 'We didn't pull iron till they did.'

'You can believe him, Burch,' said Freestone. 'I never saw 'em face to face before, but I've seen pictures and I remember their names. They're outlaw-fighters.' He gestured to the dead men. 'None of these jaspers got it in the back.'

'Just vamoosed a little while back, huh?' prodded Stretch. 'Gone a week or more?'

'That figures,' said Larry.

'They rode for me, so maybe I'm responsible for — whatever reason you had for hunting 'em,' frowned Kelsey.

'If I believed that, my partner and me'd have you covered right now,' retorted Larry. 'No, Mister Kelsey, somebody else set up the dirty deal they mixed into.' Rancher, ramrod and young Kelsey listened without interrupting while he gave a terse account of recent events in a small town. They winced and exchanged glances as he reported the burning spree and his and Stretch's close call. In conclusion, he pointed to the dead Jard Horner. 'He's the one heard us beggin' to be let out of the jail while it burned around us.'

'You know that for a fact?' asked Freestone.

'He had a special kind of laugh,' winced Stretch.

'He laughed when he heard us,' muttered Larry. "Stay and fry,' he hollered back at us. Twice we heard him laugh. That time — and right here.'

'No use blamin' yourself, Burch,' said Freestone. 'We ain't mind-readers. When we're hirin', how can we tell if a stranger's lyin'?'

Clem Kelsey was young and curious, also awestruck.

'You were locked in a cell? How *did* you get out?'

'The only citizens left in town were a couple women,' Larry told him. 'One of 'em sick, the other one tendin' her. The sick one died. The other one toted her out of a place that was burnin', then came and risked her life to turn us loose.'

'Just made it, kid,' Stretch said sombrely. 'Her duds caught fire.'

'Holy Moses!' breathed Clem.

'But she's got savvy,' said Stretch. 'Would've got blistered bad, would've burned — and us too — if she hadn't had savvy enough to flop and roll on her blazin' skirts.'

The rancher was silent a moment.

Then, 'You'll be delivering your prisoner and these dead men to the country sheriff.' He didn't voice this as a question. 'When you do, if the sheriff's leery of you, tell him Burch Kelsey will back your story next time he's in town. And you can be sure I'll do that.'

'How far . . . ?' began Larry.

'Head straight south from here,' offered Freestone. 'In an hour, you'll sight the railroad tracks. You can follow 'em clear to the county seat, Davistown. Ought to make it before sundown.'

'Yeah, much obliged,' nodded Larry. He fished out a dime and glanced at his partner. 'Heads you fetch our horses and I tie these bastards on their critters, tails the other way round.'

Before he could flip the coin, Clem asked, 'Where'd you leave your horses?' Larry told him. 'I'll go fetch 'em for you.'

'Do that, son,' urged his father, and the young man wheeled his pony and hustled it out of the clearing. 'Valentine, the sheriff's Owen Heenan and he deals square with everybody, but I have to warn you I've heard him speak of you trouble-shooters.'

'Aw, hell,' sighed Stretch.

'Real fire-eater, Heenan,' grinned the foreman.

'Given an excuse, I think it'd please Owen mightily to lock you up,' cautioned Kelsey. 'Why give him any reason? I said he deals square. You answer his questions the way you explained everything to me, no foolery, no jokes nor backtalk, and he'll be reasonable enough. You don't *have* to rile him do you?'

'We sure appreciate the advice,' said Larry. 'And we'll heed it, believe me.'

Freestone was helping the Texans secure bodies to horses when young Clem returned leading the sorrel and pinto. Befuddled, not yet fully conscious, Dansley was boosted astride the fourth Rafter K animal and his hands tied to the saddlehorn, his boots lashed to stirrups. Stretch retrieved the bullet-holed derby and planted it on his head, causing him to loose a groan of anguish; that groan wasn't likely to earn him any sympathy.

As they made to start for the south of the clearing, Larry leading the animal toting Dansley, Stretch the death-horses, Kelsey called after them.

'You can tell Sheriff Heenan I'll be in town a couple of days from now.'

Pushing south from Rafter K an hour later, the trouble-shooters cocked ears to Dansley's shocked oaths. He could see clearly now, and understand his situation, three more of his cronies dead, he a prisoner of the men who knew too much. Abruptly, he abandoned profanity and resorted to bluster.

'A smart lawyer'll blow holes through any accusations you make against me!'

'You forgettin' we spied on you bastards before we showed ourselves?' growled Larry. 'Tinhorn, he'd have to be the smartest lawyer in the whole damn country. You'd do better for yourself by givin' me some answers.'

'I'll tell you nothing,' snarled Dansley. 'And I'll deny everything.'

'Eight of you hit Curran and set it afire,' drawled Stretch. 'Only three of you still breathin'. Still think it was a smart deal, dude, gettin' tricked up as horse soldiers?'

'This ain't your best day,' taunted Larry. 'Biggest mistake you and your lowdown buddies ever made. Had to have your fun, burn the town. Wasn't enough you got what you were there for — Zack Dryden's cashbox. When you sonsabitches started fires, the town wasn't empty, but you never stopped to think.'

'And didn't care a damn anyway,' accused Stretch.

'Want to tell us where you buried Todd Melrose — or *if* you buried him?' demanded Larry. 'Mightn't matter to you, but his uncle'd like to know.'

He wasn't glancing backward, nor was Stretch looking at Dansley at this moment, so neither drifter caught

Dansley's puzzled expression. He stared at them a moment, then said curtly, 'I don't know what you're talking about — and that's all I intend saying.'

He was maintaining his silence when, at noon, after following the railroad south for several hours, his captors called a halt by a small waterhole. There was good grass for the horses, who rested while the Texans gathered wood and cooked a meagre lunch. They spoon-fed their prisoner before re-securing him to his horse.

It was 4.15 p.m. when they sighted the county seat, a bigger than most cattletown on the north-south rail route; they had made good time. A few minutes after their arrival, Sheriff Owen Heenan's pre-supper libation at the Happy Lady Saloon on Main Street was interrupted by one of his deputies, the lean and wiry Vince Judd. Heenan was a veteran lawman and muscular, broad-faced and grey-eyed, sporting a well-tended spade beard.

'I'm not available,' he said before

Judd could address him. 'Whatever you want me for, it can wait till after supper. From here, my next stop's the Montoya Cantina for supper with the mayor.'

'Sorry, but I don't reckon so,' said Judd.

'What do you mean — you don't reckon so?' demanded Heenan.

'They're waitin' at the office,' said Judd. 'They brought in a live prisoner, gamblin' man from Parera, and three dead cowhands — on Rafter K horses. I had old Saul lock up the live one. Pike took the stiffs to the funeral parlor.'

'Gun trouble?' frowned Heenan.

'On Rafter K range,' nodded Judd. 'They claim Kelsey'll be in town in a couple days to back their story.'

'Who're *they*?' Heenan wanted to know. 'We talking about Federals or bounty hunters or what? And how many of 'em?'

'Just two,' Judd said carefully, and he wondered if he should retreat out of arm's reach of his boss. 'Texans and plenty tall. We got a file on 'em.'

'Not . . . ?' began Heenan.

'Sorry, but yes,' said Judd. 'Those troubleshooters — Valentine and Emerson.'

Heenan's eyes gleamed. He swore softly, drained his glass and started for the batwings with Judd at his heels. Downtown they walked briskly for two blocks, then up the steps to the law office porch and into the sheriff's headquarters to find the notorious hell-raisers seated before the main desk with their Stetsons in their laps. At once, they rose and accorded the boss-lawman respectful nods and a polite greeting.

'Evenin', Sheriff Heenan,' said Larry.

'Pardon us if we're intrudin', Sheriff suh,' Stretch apologized. 'The thing is, we got no choice on account of we're plumb law-abidin'.'

'Brought in a prisoner and three stiffs,' explained Larry. 'So you're gonna want to know how come and,

174

whenever you're ready, I'll be glad to tell you everything.'

The county jailer, Saul Bowker, was well on in years, lined of face and rheumy-eyed. He lounged in the jailhouse doorway, thumbs hooked into the armholes of his vest, his old Navy Colt holstered two inches west of his navel, studying the tall men curiously. Heenan eyed them warily and in overt disapproval as he sank into his desk chair. The Texans promptly reseated themselves, fished out Bull Durham and matches, but did not begin building cigarettes before requesting and being granted his permission. Heenan resented this show of courtesy; things weren't happening as per his expectations.

'All right,' he said sharply. 'Let's hear it.'

He heard it all. Everything that had happened to the Texans from the moment of their riding into Curran, every detail up to this moment was related by Larry in less than fifteen minutes. Only one omission. He had decided Heenan did not need to know that five dead killers had been relieved of every paper dollar they were toting at the time of their demise.

When he had finished, the jailer, summoned by Dansley, retreated into the cell-block. Judd had been joined by the other deputy, red-haired Pike Whiddon. They filled the outer doorway, impressed and close-mouthed, while their boss stared hard at the trouble-shooters and announced,

'If I'm to be custodian of a man accused of looting, arson and attempted murder, I'll need a signed statement, everything you've told me put on paper in the form of an affidavit and duly recorded and witnessed by a justice of the peace.'

'Sure,' nodded Larry. 'I'll be glad to oblige.'

'Us peace-lovin' travellers always do our doggonedest to work along with the law,' Stretch said virtuously.

Heenan sighed heavily.

'Judd, go ask Luther Moss to join us.'

Judd hurried away. Bowker emerged from the cell-block to report,

'The sorehead wants paper and somethin' to write with.'

'Broke down, did he?' prodded Heenan. 'Wants to confess?'

'Nope,' grunted the jailer. 'Wants to write a letter. To get money enough for hirin' a big shot lawyer?'

'That's his privilege — much good it'll do him,' shrugged Heenan. 'Take him a pad and an envelope and the inkpot and — not *that* pen, you old goat. That's mine. He can have the one that scratches.'

'If I'm an old goat,' Bowker retorted while helping himself to the writing materials, 'you're a sore-assed bull.'

'He can get away with that,' Heenan informed the Texans. 'Happens to be my uncle. It's what you mavericks're getting away with that breaks my heart. You're a helluva disappointment, both of you.'

'Well, shucks, we're tryin' to do this right,' protested Stretch. 'Ain't sassed you, spat on your floor, helped ourselves to your booze . . . '

'That's the disappointment,' complained Heenan.

'Pardon us all to hell,' Larry said with a wry gin.

'If you knew how long I've hungered to have you thrown into my jail . . . ' began Heenan.

'Long time, huh?' Larry asked sympathetically.

'Ten years or more,' grouched Heenan. 'After all I've heard about the law officers you've treated as jackasses, all the helling around, all your heavy-handed, wanton disruption of the peace, here you sit, so damn respectful, so co-operative, a couple of do-righters on your best behaviour. Why am I being spared your insolence? That's a straight question, so I think it rates a straight answer.'

'Better be you gives the straight answer, runt,' urged Stretch. 'If I tried,

178

I'd likely make a hash of it.'

'Straight answer, Sheriff,' offered Larry. 'We choose our targets. Burch Kelsey calls you a square-dealer, and we never rile an honest lawman.'

'First it's courtesy,' sighed Heenan, 'then it's compliments.'

Luther Moss, J.P., returned with Judd and equipped with affidavits and his own writing materials. He suggested to the sheriff that Larry dictate his deposition. Heenan agreed and so did Larry, who intended dictating no faster than it was taking Dansley to write a letter. He had plans for the letter and, had Heenan or Stretch suspected his plan, Heenan might have suffered a seizure. As for Stretch — well — he would be more than a little agitated, but later.

When Bowker came out of the cell-block again, he showed Heenan a sealed and addressed envelope. Larry watched him toss it into a flat wire basket, oblong shaped, at Heenan's left.

He finished his statement; he and

his partner then put their names to it and the J.P. witnessed their signatures and added his seal. It then occurred to Larry to remark to the sheriff, 'Sizeable town you got here.'

'The railroad brings growth, you know that,' said Heenan.

'Newspaper here?' asked Larry.

'The *County Herald* — what about it?' challenged Heenan.

'Two of the smart operators that burned Curran're still free,' Larry reminded him. 'My partner and me, we aim to track 'em down.'

'I already guessed that,' said Heenan. 'Make your point.'

'Why warn 'em?' shrugged Larry. 'Do your local scribblers have to know Dansley's name? Is there some law says you got to give 'em everything I gave you?' He glanced at Bowker and the deputies, then stared hard at Moss. 'Our chances'll be better if . . .'

'No publicity, huh?' frowned Heenan.

'Might help.' said Larry.

Heenan thought about that while

180

matching stares with the others.

'You're no blabbermouth, Luther, right?'

'I can keep a secret,' said the J.P., 'if advised to do so.'

'That's what I'm advising,' nodded Heenan. 'Vince, Pike, Saul?'

'Whatever you say,' offered Judd. 'You're the boss.'

'All right, Valentine,' said Heenan. 'You've cooperated, and now I'm cooperating. Satisfied?'

'Muchas gracias,' acknowledged Larry.

He nudged Stretch and, as they got to their feet, Heenan warily enquired, 'You staying long here?'

'Nope.' Larry raised a hand reassuringly. 'No longer'n we have to. Be out of Davistown before you know it.'

They were moving to the street door when Heenan took the five letters from his correspondence tray and held them out to Deputy Whiddon.

'Pike, you'd better drop these off at the Postal Telegraph office.'

Minutes later, Stretch was demanding to be told, 'Why're we taggin' that deputy?'

'He's takin' mail to be sent out,' muttered Larry. 'Includin' Dansley's letter.'

'So?' frowned Stretch.

'I get that letter, maybe I'll know where to find Miller, the smart hombre that set up the Curran thing,' explained Larry.

Stretch eyed him sidelong.

'We can't do that! Hell's sakes, runt, we've never messed with the U.S. Mail!'

'There's a first time for everything,' Larry said calmly. 'Quit frettin'. I got a good reason that makes sense, so it ain't gonna bother me none.'

'No? Well, it's sure gonna bother *me*.'

'Won't bother you at all. You'll just do what you got to do, while I do what I got to do.'

'And — uh — what do I got to do?'

'You mean you ain't guessed?'

'No, I ain't guessed!'

'Well, we tag the deputy into the Postal Telegraph. He puts Heenan's mail wherever they put it and moseys out again. Then, while you cover me, I sneak that one letter off the pile, meanin' the one Dansley wrote.'

'How am I gonna . . . ?'

'Think of somethin'. Just keep the postmaster busy long enough for me to grab the letter.'

'Holy Hannah!'

'You can do it.'

'That's what *you* say.'

In a state of high trepidation, the taller Texan followed his partner into the Postal Telegraph office in time to see Deputy Whiddon toss the letters into a tray on a side counter, a tray similar to the one on his boss's desk. The deputy then departed and, by fortunate coincidence, the only other locals now on hand were the postmaster, Arnold Chester, and his wife, the latter in her going out attire, adjusting her artificial berry-festooned hat and informing him, 'This *is* my night for supper with the church committee ladies. If you've forgotten, that's your problem.'

'I eat supper too,' grouched Chester.

'It's on the stove,' she shrugged. 'You aren't helpless, Arnold. All you have to do is spoon it off the skillet onto a plate. You should complain?'

Atop the pile was the letter written and addressed by Dansley, and Larry figured now was his best chance. He nudged Stretch, who summoned his courage and launched the necessary diversion, advancing on the couple and at once winning their attention, all of it; Larry might as well have been elsewhere.

'Sadie!' he cried. 'Sadie Corkhill — after all these years of searchin'! And, doggone it, you ain't changed a bit, just as purty as ever!'

'Beg pardon?' blinked Mrs Chester.

'Who're you calling Sadie?' challenged the postmaster. 'Mister, this is . . . '

'Sadie!' beamed Stretch. 'I'd know you anywhere!'

Larry was at the side counter, the Chesters oblivious to him, he sneaking the item of mail out of the basket and secreting it inside his shirt.

'I swear I don't know . . . ' began Mrs Chester.

'It's me, honey!' Stretch spread his arms. 'Your old beau from Quinn's Fork back in Texas, me, Woody. Don't you remember me — how I used to carry your books to school?'

'I've never seen this man before in my life,' she protested to her husband.

'Let me set you straight, Woody, or whatever you call yourself,' frowned Chester. 'You're talking to my wife and her name's Louisa and, before we got married, her family name sure wasn't Corkhill. It was O'Grady. Can't you see you've made a mistake?'

'She — ain't Sadie?' Stretch appeared crest-fallen. 'But — she's a dead ringer for . . . '

'Lou's never been in Texas — have

you, Lou?' demanded Chester. His wife shook her head. 'How long ago, Mister?'

'Uh — well — we were just kids,' mumbled Stretch.

'Well, come on now,' chided Chester. 'That had to be a long time back a good long time.'

'Thank you, Arnold Chester, and you're no spring chicken either,' bridled Louisa.

Finding Larry suddenly beside him, Stretch decided to deal him in.

'The lady ain't Sadie,' he said mournfully.

'No, I can see that,' nodded Larry. 'Ain't blamin' you for takin' her for Sadie, mind. The lady must've looked a lot like her.' He smoothly apologized on his partner's behalf. 'Hope you good folks'll pardon my friend's mistake.'

'I guess anybody can made a mistake,' shrugged Chester.

'One thing you can believe, ma'am,' offered Larry. He doffed his Stetson, a courtesy promptly imitated by Stretch.

'My friend sure didn't insult you, mistakin' you for Sadie. It's more a compliment.' To Chester, he explained, 'The Corkhills were a mighty fine family, God-fearin', respectable folks.'

'I'll take your word for that,' said Chester.

'No offense, ma'am,' mumbled Stretch.

'None taken,' Louisa said impatiently. 'But now I have to hurry or I'll be late for the committee supper.'

She went her way, after which Chester gave Stretch a bad moment by asking,

'Why are you here? You didn't see my wife till you walked in, so you must've wanted something.'

'I — uh . . . ' began Stretch.

'Trains,' said Larry. 'Here to ask about trains. I already guessed you send the mail by the railroad, so . . . '

'Depends on the addresses,' said Chester. 'To places east and west, Wells Fargo delivers it. North or south, the railroad, sure. Mailsack in the caboose.'

He gestured to several mailbags. 'Clerk from the depot'll pick it up before the northbound leaves tomorrow morning, then the rest around noon in time to load it on the southbound. That all you want to know? I'm late for my supper.'

'Us too,' said Larry. 'Much obliged.'

'I don't know why you couldn't have asked at the railroad depot,' frowned Chester.

'Now why didn't *I* think of that?' Larry chided himself as they walked out.

When they were well clear of the Postal Telegraph, Stretch grimaced and began grouching.

'Next time you get such a notion . . . '

'You did fine,' shrugged Larry. 'What matters is I got the letter.'

They returned to the hitchrail fronting the sheriff's office for their horses and led them to another close by a Mexican cafe. The Estoban establishment boasted private dining-rooms, and privacy was what Larry craved right now. Heaping helpings of chili con carne were served them, after which Larry told the swarthy waitress they would alert her when ready for coffee.

He downed a few mouthfuls before slipping the envelope from inside his shirt. As he did so, he was conscious of other paper stashed between that garment and the top half of his underwear. Stretch patted his own chest and muttered a reminder.

'We keep collectin' greenbacks every time we get shot at.'

'Ain't that the truth,' Larry agreed, tearing the envelope's flap, slipping the folded sheets out. 'I'm gonna have to get somethin' to tote it in, a sack, another wallet, somethin'.'

He took careful note of the address on the envelope.

'Anson Miller, Esq.,
Grand Union Casino,
Battery Street,
San Francisco, California.'

'Miller.' Stretch nudged his memory again. 'They talked of a hombre name of Miller while we spied on 'em. Sounded like he's the polecat planned the whole dirty deal. And him and a another hombre . . . '

'I think they called him Watling,' said Larry.

'Yup,' grunted Stretch. 'Him and Watling only took Carrie Dryden's beads and let Dansley and the others share the twenty-five thousand.'

'Give me time to read this,' said Larry.

'Who's stoppin' you?' shrugged Stretch, plying his fork again.

Dansley hadn't written the customary 'Dear' before the name Anson. The letter read:

'If you refuse to help me, I swear I will try for indemnity by spilling all I know to the law. Bud, Joe and the other three are dead, which leaves just you, me and Hal, and somebody got wise to the whole deal.

I have been arrested, but a good lawyer, the kind who does not come cheap, could maybe get me out of this fix. So you mail me $2000 cash care of the County Jail, Davistown, Davis County, New Mexico Territory — and fast — and your name will never be mentioned, your secret will be safe with me.

Too bad I have to threaten you, but I am busted, so there is no other way.

R. B. Dansley.'

Larry placed the note before Stretch and, while his partner perused it, concentrated on satisfying his hunger. The reading took Stretch twice as long. When finished, he sighed resignedly.

'Aw, hell, I can read your mind. We're gonna travel clear to 'Frisco — a real big city.'

'I don't relish it any more'n you do,' said Larry. 'But tell me how else we're gonna nail the skunk that set it all up — and maybe get back Carrie's jewellery?' He returned the note to its envelope, folded it and nudged it into his hip-pocket. 'We'll know where to find him when we get there. If I hadn't stole Dansley's letter — how d'you like the idea of us searchin' that whole damn city?'

'Not one little bit,' winced Stretch. He didn't speak again until his plate was empty. Then, 'Helluva long ride.'

'I hanker to get there muy pronto,' said Larry. 'Railroad's the fastest way. And no saddlesores.'

After supper, they rode to the railroad depot. The clerk announced that, to reach San Francisco from here the speediest way, they would need to be on tomorrow morning's northbound.

'Switch to a westbound at Santa Fe. That'll carry you all the way to San Francisco and I can issue tickets for the whole journey. One way or return?'

'We'll be comin' back,' said Larry, producing his wallet. 'Now, about our horses . . .'

'Sorry,' said the clerk. 'You depart eight forty-five sharp and it's a passenger service, no accommodation for horses. But you don't have to worry about leaving them here. I'll direct you to a livery stable where they couldn't get better care, best stable in town.'

Larry paid for their passage and, following the ticket-clerk's directions, they found the Burford stable. There, after admiring the sorrel and pinto, the genial Mexican hostler promised these fine caballos would enjoy his personal attention. Handsomely tipped, he also undertook to safeguard the Texans' saddles and other gear.

'Do that,' urged Larry. 'And we'll be just as generous when we get back.'

'Where to now?' Stretch asked as they left the stable.

'Gotta buy somethin' to tote Zack's paper cash in,' said Larry. 'Then we check into the hotel nearest the railroad depot.' His face clouded over. 'This ain't my night for poker or any kind of good time.

'Hey, all of a sudden you're miserable,' observed Stretch. 'What's fazin' you, runt?'

Larry told him, but not till he had paid for their overnight stay in a ground-floor double of a hotel a short distance from the depot. They removed hats, boots and sidearms, perched on the edges of their beds and rolled and lit cigarettes. The taller drifter then listened to his partner's grim prediction.

'We were in San Francisco years ago,' Larry said moodily. 'Now we're headed there again and I got a mean feelin' about it. You'll get out of that big town alive — but maybe I won't.'

7

Leaning On Otto Vormann

LARRY had purchased a small satchel of soft leather. Just the right size, he hoped. Into it, he packed longwise all the greenbacks from inside their shirts, the wealth salvaged from the late Bud Rettig, Joe Woodward, Slim Ringle, Jard Horner and Eddie Goff, while Stretch watched through worried eyes.

'Whatsamatter? Got a feelin' in your bones?' Larry nodded. 'C'mon, runt, you ain't gonna die in 'Frisco.'

'Didn't say I'm sure,' shrugged Larry.

'No chance,' said Stretch. 'I'll be right with you, just like always.'

'That could mean we'd both end up in a big city graveyard,' complained Larry. He grimaced in disgust. 'What

195

a way to go. Couple Texas mavericks like us.'

'My bones don't feel like your bones do,' declared Stretch, always the optimist. 'We don't cotton to 'Frisco nor any other lit up, hustlin' city, but we ain't gonna let it lick us. Take it from me, ol' buddy, we'll get out of there alive after we settle our business with Number Seven and Number Eight of them fake soldiers and find out where they left poor Todd. If they didn't plant Todd, we'll plant him, and then we'll take Zack's fortune home to him. That's how it's gonna be, and don't you never doubt it, hear?'

'At least we know who to look for,' Larry said grimly.

They carried only Larry's saddlebags into a Pullman of the northbound ten minutes before departure time next morning. The satchel fitted snugly into a saddlebag, as snugly as Larry's hip-wallet and the gunbelts girding their loins, the tied-down holstered .45s.

Upon their arrival in Santa Fe, they

were told they would wait only an hour before transferring to a train bound for the west coast. That meant San Francisco to them and a confrontation with the architect of the outrage inflicted on a small town — Anson Miller of the Grand Union Casino, a place that should not be hard to find, even in a city of such size.

★ ★ ★

Mid-afternoon of the day of the westbound's scheduled arrival in San Francisco, two representatives of that city's police force were giving jeweller Otto Vormann some bad moments. Vormann was dapper and blunt-featured, a man of slight physique, an opportunist from way back. And, right now, he was being intimidated quietly, relentlessly, by a couple of experts.

Being big city law officers, these plainclothesmen bore little resemblance to the county sheriffs and town marshals of the still untamed frontiers to the east. Sergeant Pat Gerhane was hefty, six feet tall and hard-eyed. His townsuit had not been custom-made, but fitted him to perfection. His aide, Detective Dave Kosleck, was dark and shorter, barrel-chested, the set of his shoulders and chin suggesting that, in a brawl with waterfront low life, he could be as tough a slugger as his immediate superior.

The scene was Vormann's private office above his store in one of the big town's best areas. He was shrinking into the chair behind his desk. Neither of his hard-boiled visitors had accepted his invitation to be seated. They stood over him, doing their talking softly but compellingly and from around half-smoked cigars.

'Really, Sergeant Gerhane . . . ' Vormann strove in vain to present an unruffled exterior, 'I'm at a loss to understand the purpose of your questions.'

'The hell you are, Otto,' grinned Gerhane.

'You understand good, Dutch,' muttered Kosleck. 'We handed you a search warrant and you read it. If you don't get the point . . . ' He shook his head sceptically. 'No, you couldn't be that dumb.'

'I don't deal in . . . ' began Vormann.

'Save the bull,' sneered Gerhane. 'You think Chief of Detectives O'Keefe bosses a squad of lamebrains? Hell, Otto, this place of yours has been under surveillance for so long — if you knew how long, your eyes'd pop.'

'Funny how it always seems to happen,' remarked Kosleck. He moved to the desk, squatted on its inner corner and reached down to adjust the jeweller's cravat and flick an imaginary speck of dust from his lapel. 'Damnedest thing, Dutch. Some Nob Hill mansion gets burglarized and — surprise, surprise — a little while afterward some thief well-known to the Department pays a call on you.'

As Vormann began sweating, Gerhane said genially, 'Not right through the street entrance to your elegant showroom, Otto. Hell, no. Door off the back alley and right up that little stairway to the balcony outside your window.'

'They leave the same way,' said Kosleck.

'A lot of 'em,' nodded Gerhane. 'Familiar faces, Otto, with familiar names. We know 'em all. Of course they don't have to bust the lock on *your* window. You don't lock it. You expect 'em. They're regular visitors.'

'Which side of this fence should I sit on?' quipped Kosleck. 'Our friend here's gonna flop right out of his chair if I don't steady him.'

'So steady him, Dave,' requested Gerhane. 'I think you'll find that decanter contains high quality booze, cognac probably.'

A stiff swig did nothing to ease Vormann's apprehension. He tried a bold front, but his voice shook.

'I'm just a dealer in rare gems and objet d'art,' he protested. 'When I purchase — various items — I assume

I'm not buying stolen property.' Gerhane yawned. Pointedly. Vormann flushed resentfully. 'See here, Sergeant . . . !'

'Shut up and listen,' growled Gerhane. 'No more fooling around. Man to man, okay? You could be in big trouble, more than you can handle, and you know it. How much trouble? Well, that's up to you. The Department might go easy on you, give you a break. Of course there'd be conditions. The way you've been operating, we call it working against us.'

'I have always respected and obeyed the law,' pleaded Vormann.

'I'm running short on patience, Pat,' scowled Kosleck. 'The hell with him. If he insults our intelligence one more time . . . '

'Take it easy,' soothed Gerhane. 'Let's stick to procedure, Dave. We don't beat up on 'em, don't strongarm 'em or use our pistols unless we're under threat. And Otto's no threat to us, are you, Otto? Use your handkerchief, Otto. You're sweating into your collar now, and that looks disgusting. Where was I?'

'Warning this bum he's been working against us,' offered Kosleck.

'Oh, sure,' nodded Gerhane. 'Now, Otto, it goes like this. You want the department off your back, here's what you do from now on. Some miscreant tries a back window deal, offers you a few baubles, like brooches, rings, a string of pearls for instance, you stall, understand? Hold the stuff, tell him check back in a few hours — then you tip us. You got that?'

'Hasn't that always been my custom?' Vormann said defensively.

'No, it hasn't!' snapped Kosleck.

'You want him to faint?' chided Gerhane. 'What can he tell us if he's unconscious?'

'I'll try hard to keep my hands off him,' sighed Kosleck. 'Too bad we're on duty. That cognac looks good.'

'You understand what I've been saying. Otto?' challenged Gerhane. Vormann winced and nodded. 'Fine.

Feel better already, don't you? See how easy it's gonna be? You be reasonable, we'll be reasonable. We scratch your back, you scratch ours.'

'I'm an honest businessman and always willing to co-operate with . . . ' began Vormann.

'That's nice,' approved Gerhane.

'Just beautiful,' said Kosleck. 'Gives us a warm feeling inside.'

'So here's where you start co-operating,' Gerhane told the jeweller. 'I'm getting to be curious about a citizen we caught onto recently. You'll remember his name. Anson Miller. Doesn't seem that long ago he was doing a little bunko around our fair city, just penny ante stuff, but naturally this brought him to my attention. Since then, just lately in fact, a fancy new joint opens on Battery Street.'

'Called the Grand Union Casino,' said Kosleck. 'Soft music, champagne, games of chance. And hostesses yet. Not whores, mind you. High-class.'

'The place caters strictly for the

carriage trade,' said Gerhane. 'And who do you suppose owns and manages it?'

'Surprise, surprise,' grinned Kosleck.

'The same Anson Miller,' said Gerhane. 'And, how do you like this for a coincidence? We wondered how Miller managed to finance such an expensive layout — until I remembered *he* was one of your sneak visitors, the kind who try hard not to be seen climbing your back stairs.'

Vormann took another mouthful of cognac, got it down and regained some, not all, of his composure.

'I know that particular gentleman, yes,' he said. 'There was a transaction, certainly, and I don't doubt the price I paid was more than enough to finance his acquisition and redecoration of a building on Battery Street. It was, you see, a very special item, so the figure was high. But I saw no reason for suspicion. I was, of course, unaware the police were interested in him.'

'What was his pitch?' demanded

Kosleck. 'How'd he say he came by the item?'

'He inherited it from his grandmother,' frowned Vormann. 'For five years or more, Mister Miller was so overawed by its obvious value that he kept it in a safety deposit box at a bank. However, upon deciding to go into business, he decided to dispose of the necklace to the highest bidder.'

'Meaning you,' said Gerhane. 'Special you said. *How* special?'

'A necklace of rare design,' said Vormann. 'Emeralds and rubies, all the metal work pure gold.'

'So, already, you got your workroom staff breaking it up.' guessed Kosleck. 'Selling the sparklers as separate items, you'll double what you paid Miller.'

'No.' Vormann shook his head earnestly. 'To damage that necklace would be vandalism. I could never permit it. No, indeed. It will be guarded with the respect it deserves until I find the right buyer. I will realize a handsome profit, but that's my right as a marketer of . . . '

'So you still got it?' prodded Gerhane.

'I've said so,' nodded Vormann.

'In there?' asked Gerhane, his gaze fixing on the safe in the rear corner.

'Well, hardly,' said Vormann. 'Pieces of such value are kept in the basement vault, which has a combination lock.'

'I'm getting *very* curious,' declared Gerhane, snapping his fingers. 'So off your butt, Otto. Take us down there. I want to see what Miller sold you.'

The detectives were taken to the vault where they inspected the necklace. Vormann became anxious. If this recent purchase proved to be stolen property, he would suffer a heavy loss. Knowing Vormann to be one of San Francisco's wealthiest citizens, Gerhane offered no sympathy, just an order. On no account should Vormann dispose of the necklace. He could consider himself its custodian for the time being. Kosleck added a warning. Vormann shouldn't even *dream* of having his staff fashion a replica. Still intimidated, the jeweller promised to await further instructions from the San Francisco PD.

As the detectives began a slow stroll back to Police Headquarters, Kosleck lit a fresh cigar and asked,

'Think we can trust him?'

'*Now* we can trust him,' opined Gerhane. 'Sure, from now on. Remember, Dave, there's more than one way to skin a cat or scare hell out of a sharp operator like that Dutchman.'

'The psychological approach and the cunning of the Irish,' grinned Kosleck, American-born of Polish parentage.

'I think we were both reading his mind,' said Gerhane.

'Reading his mind was easy,' shrugged Kosleck. 'A guy like Vormann would lose his shirt, his pants too, playing poker. It's all there on his sweating kisser, everything he's thinking.'

'He was seeing prison bars, Dave,' said Gerhane. 'Thinking of the company he'd have to keep, the food he'd have to eat. It wouldn't be his style of cuisine. Even a short hitch in a state pen would be too much for him.'

'So how do you figure this Miller guy?' frowned Kosleck.

'Got to be a bad one,' decided Gerhane. 'If he's straight, so's a dog's hind legs. If his grandmother willed him that treasure, my grandmother — back in County Cork — willed me the crown jewels of England. But proving my suspicious, getting an iron-clad case on him, is something else.'

'We stay after him, right?' prodded Kosleck.

'Just as hot as me, are you?' grinned Gerhane.

'Hotter,' growled Kosleck. 'I hate for crooks to be richer than law-abiding citizens. It hurts my feelings, Pat. I develop a lousy disposition, and that's rough on Martha. She's a good wife and deserves better.'

'When we get back to the office, let's both ask around,' said Gerhane. 'I'll try for a few minutes of the captain's time and shoot a few ideas at him. We'll talk to beat cops, every member of the detective squad we can find, any fellow-officers who might know anything about Miller or his place of business.

'Any dick with ideas,' mused Kosleck.

'Ideas, hunches, suggestions,' nodded Gerhane. 'I'm so hot for a lead on Mister Anson Miller, I'll settle for whatever I can get.'

★ ★ ★

Stretch, seated by a window of the westbound's second Pullman car, thrust his head out to stare ahead, withdrew it and grimaced resentfully.

'I can see a big piece of it already,' he muttered. 'We'll be there pretty soon.'

'Yep,' grunted Larry. 'Railroad's mightly reliable. Trains most always arrive on time.'

'Ever hear of fishes out of water?' challenged Stretch.

'I know what it means,' said Larry.

'That's how we're gonna feel,' Stretch predicted. 'The minute we mosey out of that big depot.'

'We won't let it throw us,' said Larry.

'Just so I'll be ready, what's our first move?'

'Well, it's for sure we won't get it done and quit all on the same night, so we're gonna have to check into a hotel.'

'Not far from the depot, huh? Else we're apt to get lost. That's the trouble with big towns, Denver, 'Frisco, Chicago, any of 'em. A man can get lost 'fore he knows it.'

'It'll be close to the depot.'

'We gonna eat before we . . . ?'

'Uh huh. We'll eat. And right after supper, we'll start doin' what we came here to do.'

'You still spooked about us havin' to be in this big city?' asked Stretch.

Only to his close amigo of better than two decades would Larry confide such disquiet.

'Still spooked. It don't set right with me.'

'I savvy how you feel, runt,' said Stretch, and he did. 'Ridin' the plains, travellin' mountain country, stoppin' by mine camps and cattletowns, we know our way around, know how to handle any trouble comes our way. Different in big cities. Too many people, too many streets and us never knowin' how far they'll take us. Too much light.'

'Too many sharpers,' said Larry. 'If they ain't tryin' to pick your pocket, they're jumpin' you, haulin' you into an alley to bust your head and grab your bankroll. There's more badge-toters than we'd find in any trail town — police I've heard 'em called. Police. Cops. And somethin' else I've heard, must've heard it from a city man. Where're the cops when you most need 'em?'

'Amigo, no sonofabitch is gonna pick our pockets nor jump us,' soothed Stretch.

'They'll bleed if they try it,' scowled Larry.

'Look, we're a couple pilgrims from

way back there where everything's wide open, but we ain't rubes,' Stretch said encouragingly. 'We still got savvy, we still hit hard and we only left our Winchesters back in Davistown, not our hoglegs. Smile, Larry. Forget about dyin' in 'Frisco.'

'You listenin' to yourself?' Larry demanded with a wry grin.

'What'd I say?' blinked Stretch.

'Forget about dyin',' said Larry. 'Damn it, that's somethin' we *never* forget. Nobody lives forever. Only reason we're still alive and healthy is, when the chips're down, we always know it's gonna be them — the bastards tryin' to gun us down — or us. We keep that in mind when we defend ourselves. If we didn't, we'd've been fillin' six foot holes fifteen, twenty years ago.'

'Well . . . ' shrugged Stretch.

'Don't get me wrong,' said Larry. 'I ain't made up my mind I'm gonna stop a bullet in this big city. I'm just leery is all. And, when it matters most, I aim to be mighty careful.'

The train steamed to a halt on schedule and the tall men donned their Stetsons to follow other passengers from the car, Larry toting his saddle-bags. Quitting the biggest railroad depot they had ever seen, they paused, bedazzled by the lights of San Francisco, intimidated by the volume of traffic in the immediate vicinity. It was a long pause. They waited to get their bearings and, before daring the traffic, focussed with care on the lamplit shingle of a triple-storied building, the Madigan Hotel.

Drivers of cabs, surreys, every kind of horse-drawn vehicle, aimed abuse at them as they dodged their way across a busy thoroughfare, always with that lamplit shingle in sight. Reaching it, they entered the lobby panting and were sized up by the shirtsleeved man behind the reception desk.

They asked about accommodation and were heartened by his response. He grinned amiably and his accent was encouragingly familiar, unmistakably a southern drawl.

'Texas is where you're from, and don't tell me I'm not right.'

'Friend, you sure ain't wrong,' said Stretch. 'How about you? Carolina?'

'Alabama. Phin Madigan's the name.' Madigan offered his hand. 'I own this place. That's my excuse for bein' here, but no reason for stayin'. I'll give 'Frisco a couple more years, I reckon, then sell up and head for home, Orden's Crossin' on the east bank of the old Cahaba River.' After shaking their hands, he turned the register toward them. 'What's your pleasure? Like a double or a couple side by side singles? Number Eleven, second floor, could suit you fine. Two right fine beds. We put brand-new mattresses on 'em just yesterday.'

'Sounds good, Phin,' said Larry, inking the pen. He signed the register, then glimpsed the safe just beyond the open doorway of the room behind Madigan. 'That safe. Good lock?'

'Combination type,' shrugged Madigan. 'Key locks're too easy for a thief to pick. Don't fret, boys. If you got stuff you want me to put in my safe, it'll still be there when I open it again. And, before the wife and me call it a day, we lock this place tight. How d'you want to pay? By the day, by the week . . . ?'

'Don't plan on stayin' long,' said Larry, passing the pen to his partner. 'I'll pay you for one night. If we got to linger longer, I'm good for the extra.'

Madigan named his rates. Larry paid him while Stretch signed the register. He then proffered a key, turned the book around to glance at their signatures and loosed a low whistle.

'Well, I'll be . . . !'

'They got newspapers in big cities,' Stretch reminded Larry.

'*Specially* in big cities,' grouched Larry.

'Listen . . . ' Madigan dropped his voice as Larry removed his and Stretch's shaving gear from a saddlebag and rebuckled the flap, 'I call this a real honor, you boys choosin' my place.

But — uh — you're many a long mile from . . . '

'As if we don't know it,' sighed Stretch.

'Tread wary, huh?' urged Madigan. 'All kinds of street trash in this man's town. They spot a couple fellers in cow-hands' rig, they peg 'em for suckers. So careful where you step, who you talk to and where you stash your bankroll, you know?'

'Muchas gracias, Phin,' said Larry.

'Pleasure's all mine, Larry — and Stretch,' grinned the hotel-keeper. 'Dinin'-room's open. You get good chow here. Goin' out after supper?'

'Got a little unfinished business to tend,' nodded Larry.

'I'll still be here,' said Madigan. 'Anything you need, directions to where you want to go, anything like that, I can help.

Larry surrendered his saddlebags and watched Madigan secure them in his safe, then climbed the stairs with his partner. They let themselves into

Room 11, second floor, opened the window and traded glances.

'We eat first,' Stretch reminded him.

'Then we get started,' said Larry.

After shaving, they checked the loading of their sidearms, donned their Stetsons, closed and locked the window and killed the lamp. Supper in the dining-room was to their taste. Tension, expectations of impending violence and their being far from their natural habitat could not dull their appetites. They ate their fill, downed two cups of coffee apiece, collected their hats and moved out to the lobby to talk to a new friend again.

'Grand Union Casino — you know it?' asked Larry.

'Heard of it, never patronized it,' drawled Madigan. 'Too rich for my blood.'

'It's on Battery Street,' said Larry. 'Would that be far from here?'

'Too far for you to hoof it, boys,' said Madigan. 'This your first time in the big city?'

'We were here before, quite a time back,' said Stretch.

'So one thing you'll recall,' suggested Madigan. 'Paved sidewalks make for miserable walkin' in your kind of boots. Better you take a cab. Plenty of 'em comin' by out front this time of night. You just wave or whistle. And — let me think now — from here to Battery Street's all of six blocks. Cost you seventy-five cents, a dollar at most. Cabman asks for more, he's tryin' to take you.'

'Thanks,' grinned Stretch. 'We'll remember.'

No sooner did they emerge from the hotel than a cab approached. Stretch crooked a finger and, reining in his horse beside them, the high-hatted, black-caped cabman offered his services.

'Take you gents somewhere?'

'You know the Grand Union Casino on Battery?' Larry asked as they climbed in.

'Know the whole town.' Plainly the

cabman thought it a foolish question. 'Got to, haven't I?'

During the crosstown journey to Battery Street, the Texans surveyed the brightly lit areas, the houses of entertainment, crowded sidewalks and tall buildings, and shared the feeling the frontier, their kind of country, was a million miles away. Fishes out of water they undoubtedly were, strangers in a strange environment, but not overawed and certainly not intimidated.

Some time later, they knew they were travelling Battery, saw the street sign. Their driver guided his horse to the sidewalk almost directly opposite a gambling house too imposing to fit the set-up of any trail-town, its facade aglow, handsome vehicles depositing representatives of the big town's upper crust out front, the men in evening attire, their wives or lady friends resplendent in silken gowns.

'That'll be eight dollars fifty,' demanded the cabman, as they alighted.

'I don't reckon so,' said Larry, tossing a silver dollar.

The cabman caught the coin and glowered at him.

'You deaf, cowboy? I said . . . '

'We hear real good,' Stretch calmly assured him. 'Ain't loco neither.'

'I calculate eighty-five cents'd be fair,' drawled Larry. 'But I'm no piker. Keep the change.'

'Come up with the rest — seven fifty — or I call a cop,' growled the cabman.

'Do that,' invited Larry. 'Maybe he'll show up before I kick your ass across the street and back again.' His eyes narrowed. 'Get goin', find a *real* sucker you can cheat.'

The cabman cursed under his breath and drove on to be promptly forgotten by the tall men now studying the Grand Union Casino.

'Big, ain't it?' remarked Stretch.

'Big and fancy,' Larry said softly. 'And it could be a high-class death-trap.'

'You still feeling . . . ?'

'Never mind how I feel.'

'Bueno. How d'you want to handle this?'

'I'm goin' in alone.'

'You're joshin' me! Think I'm gonna stay out here while you . . . ?'

'Not out here, big feller. I'll tell you where when we get there. The thing is I want you watchin' me.'

'Well, I should hope. You're liable to need back-up.'

'Just what I had in mind. Let's go.'

As they crossed toward the casino, again dodging traffic, the taller Texan said, as he had on countless other such occasions, 'Here we go again.'

'Yeah,' nodded Larry. 'Ain't that the truth.'

The Grand Union boasted a luxuriously carpeted foyer; patrons didn't just step in off the street. There was a cloak room and, some thirty feet from the street entrance, an archway through which patrons passed into the gambling area. With Stretch tagging him close, and ignoring the amused appraisal of bluebloods in the foyer, Larry advanced to the archway.

They paused there to scan the most luxuriously appointed gambling area they had even seen. Every game of chance imaginable was doing big business. There were poker parties, more than one faro table, roulette, blackjack — the Grand Union even catered to bridge and whist addicts. And the bar? Highly polished mahogany, laden shelves, mirrors all around. They were impressed, but still not overawed.

'Fine-looking staircase,' Stretch observed. 'All gold?'

'Gold paint,' said Larry. 'His private office'd be somewhere upstairs, you could make book on that. This is as far as you go, amigo. For now I mean. I'll ask for Miller at the bar, savvy? A few words from me and it's for sure he'll decide we ought to talk private.'

'And that could be plumb unhealthy for you,' frowned Stretch.

'Not with you watchin' my back,' countered Larry. 'When we climb them stairs, you stay put and keep your eyes peeled. If you spot some other hombre follow us up, that's when you move.'

'Now you're makin' sense,' approved Stretch. 'Okay, I guess we're as ready as we'll ever be.'

Oblivious to the curious stares of well-heeled folk from San Francisco's better districts, Larry started for the bar. En route, he looked to his manners, touching the brim of his Stetson to bejewelled women around whom he detoured. Then, at the bar, he waited patiently. A white-jacketed bartender eventually confronted him, raising his eyebrows.

'Mister Anson Miller — the boss,' said Larry. 'You mind pointin' me to him?'

The bartender inspected him dubiously and declared,

'Mister Miller's a very busy man.'

'That makes two of us,' said Larry.

'You want to point him out, or do I holler for him?'

'Tall gentleman with the ivory cigar-holder,' frowned the bartender. 'Over there talking to Mister and Mrs de Haven by the baccarat table.'

Larry nodded his thanks and moved in that direction. The conversation of tall and handsome Mr Miller and the de Havens ceased when the brawny man in range clothes joined them.

'You folks'll have to pardon me for buttin' in.' He doffed his Stetson to the elegant Mrs de Haven. 'I got to talk to Mister Miller and it's mighty important.'

'Really?' Miller ran an eye over him. 'Don't I have a choice, Mister . . . ?'

'You can call me Lawrence,' offered Larry. 'And I guarantee you'll want to parley.'

'We'd better leave you to it, Anson,' decided the distinguished Mr de Haven.

'Remember now, Anson,' murmured his wife, as she took his arm. 'We'll be expecting you at Delfino's Wednesday.

224

Don't disappoint us.'

'I'll be there,' promised Miller. The de Havens moved away and now he eyed Larry impatiently. 'Just what is your business with me, Lawrence?'

'I think you'd sooner we talk private,' muttered Larry.

'About what, may I ask?' demanded Miller.

'About what happened to a little town in New Mexico a while back,' said Larry. 'Place called Curran. And don't tell me you never heard of it — you and seven other hombres all tricked out as horse soldiers.'

'Never heard of the place,' shrugged Miller, his clean-cut visage devoid of expression. 'But I must confess you've aroused my curiosity. So, by all means, let's discuss it in my private office.' He beckoned. A tall man, blond and as well-tailored as he, came to them. 'Keep an eye on things, will you? This fellow's name is Lawrence, seems determined to talk to me in private about some New Mexico town — Curran.'

'Take your time,' offered the blond man. 'I'll keep everybody happy down here.'

'This way,' invited Miller, and Larry accompanied him to the stairs, cool now, too much in control to think of darting a glance over his shoulder.

When they had climbed the staircase, disappearing from Stretch's view, that wary trouble-shooter watched and waited, but only for a few moments. He saw the blond man make for the stairs, and took that as his cue.

While Miller conducted Larry to his office, while the blond man climbed the stairs, Sergeant Gerhane and Detective Kosleck were in a cab headed for the Grand Union. Their enquiries at headquarters had revealed no more than they already knew, but Gerhane wasn't letting up.

'He was a cheap bunko artist just for a little while,' he reflected. 'Then he unloads a bauble on the Dutchman and collects a bundle — so fat a bundle that he could afford to set

226

himself up as owner-manager of the fanciest gambling joint in town. So, the way I see it, it's time, Dave, time we paid a call on him and asked some questions.'

'Look, I'm not saying this is a wrong move,' frowned Kosleck. 'But how about the captain? Is O'Keefe gonna hold still for this kind of action?'

'Ever hear of rapport?' grinned Gerhane. 'We got it, we Irish, got a lot of it. Sure, I talked it over with O'Keefe, and it's fine by him — otherwise we wouldn't be headed for Battery Street right now.'

'I guess he was interested in what we learned from Vormann,' said Kosleck.

'Any captain of any detective squad would be interested in what we got from Vormann,' declared Gerhane.

After closing the door behind him, Miller sauntered to his desk and gestured for his visitor to seat himself.

'You'll find that chair is quite comfortable, Lawrence,' he said courteously. 'And now . . . ' He sank into the upholstered chair behind the desk that matched the room's other tasteful decor. 'And now, what of Curran, a place I've never heard of?'

'You know Curran,' growled Larry. 'You were there just for a day, but you sure left your mark on it.' He produced the envelope purloined from Davistown's Postal Telegraph and tossed it onto the desk. 'Maybe this'll jog your memory.'

8

Two Graves for Onete Man

LARRY wasn't a hundred percent at ease in his chair. The way it was positioned, he could watch the office door — if he dared take his eyes off Miller — but not the door connecting this room with another. He disciplined himself to study Miller's reaction to his reading of the letter.

Miller set it aside, butted his cigar and deftly removed the stub from the ivory holder.

'This letter wasn't mailed,' he frowned.

'Right,' nodded Larry. 'But Rollo Dansley sure as hell wrote it — and addressed it to you — so don't waste your time bluffin'. You're one of the eight that burned Curran and grabbed Zack Dryden's cashbox.'

'Only one way you could intercept

the letter,' said Miller. 'A serious offense, Lawrence. Highly illegal.'

'So's what you and them other buzzards did to Curran,' retorted Larry. 'And there's only one way you could know where to find Zack's stash.'

'What's your theory?' smiled Miller.

'It don't take much figurin',' scowled Larry. 'One of your scouts hung around Curran long enough to find out Zack never banked his cash. So you waited it out and, when Todd Melrose quit Curran, he played right into your hands. How'd you scare him into tellin' you the old man's secret, a knife at his throat? Maybe you stripped him and staked him on an ant heap.'

'That sounds gruesome,' said Miller, still smiling.

'Before I turn you over to the law, you're gonna tell me how to find Melrose — alive or dead,' said Larry. 'It broke their hearts, losin' their savin's and the keepsake, the necklace, but not knowin' if their nephew was buried or left for the buzzards was even worse for the Drydens, so I made 'em a promise. And I aim to keep that promise.'

Miller chuckled contemptuously and reached to a cigar-box for another Havana, reached left-handed. Following the movement, Larry felt his scalp crawl. He froze in shock, eyes riveted on the mark, the round brown spot, the birthmark, as the connecting door opened. The blond man stood there, aiming a nickel-plated pistol at his head.

'Stand up, tall man,' he ordered. 'Rise *slowly* and with your hands in front of you.'

'As usual, Hal, your timing couldn't be better,' the other man complimented him. 'If you've been listening . . . '

'With great interest,' Hal Watling assured him. 'I heard it all. Hey, Tex, you deaf? *Do* it!' Larry got to his feet, still unable to draw his gaze from the birthmark. Watling's next order was obeyed; he had no option. He slipped his holster thongs, unstrapped his belted Colt and let it drop. 'That's fine.'

'Be seated again,' offered Todd Melrose, alias Anson Miller. 'You might as well be comfortable — between now and when we dispose of you.'

'He knows a helluva lot, Anse,' frowned Watling. 'Well, could we expect a smarter move of a tinhorn like Dansley? Damn fool had to — of all things — write you a letter.'

'Don't call him Anse,' Larry said bitterly. 'He's Melrose, Todd Melrose.'

'What's he talking about?' demanded Watling.

'Quite true, Hal,' grinned Melrose. He lit his fresh cigar and taunted Larry. 'So the old folks grieve for me? Touching, quite touching.'

'They wouldn't've grieved,' muttered Larry, 'if they'd ever guessed the kind of scum they were shelterin'.'

'They bore me,' shrugged Melrose. 'The whole humdrum, self-righteous town bored me. Of course, I never let anybody suspect that. And, when I left

Curran, it was with the firm intention of returning and helping myself to the famous family heirloom. As you can imagine, I had better use for it. Hidden under that slab, it wasn't increasing in value, and that's an under-statement.'

'You're related to those Drydens?' grinned Watling. 'Boy, you sure know how to keep a secret.'

'It needn't be a secret to our inquisitive visitor,' remarked Melrose. 'I'm enjoying straightening him out, and why not? He'll learn that, as a hunch-player, he's worse than clumsy.'

'He's not leaving this room alive,' Watling said firmly.

'That's why I'm satisfying his curiosity,' said Melrose. 'Curiosity that must be driving him crazy.'

'Don't call me crazy, you sonofabitch,' countered Larry. 'No crazy man could've traced a button and a piece of cloth back to the Orion outfit, nailed Dansley and five other bastards that helped you burn Curran.'

'Burning Curran was my idea.'

bragged Melrose. 'To my way of thinking, that's all it was good for. I hated it and its people too.'

'You had to have your fun,' Larry coldly accused. 'And it never crossed your thievin' mind there might be some stayed behind after you sent the folks runnin' with your lousy lie about border raiders.'

'As Lieutenant Nolan, I think I gave a convincing performance,' chuckled Watling. 'Wish you'd heard me, Anse — I mean Todd — but of course you couldn't. It had to be you, the trooper left on the south rise to keep watch for the raiders.'

'Some stayed behind?' Melrose challenged Larry. 'You mean I was able to dispose of a citizen or two, as well as that deadly dull settlement?'

'Two women and a man,' said Larry.

'Who was the man?' asked Melrose.

'Me — stuck in the jail,' growled Larry. 'I was yellin' . . .'

'Come to think of it, I did hear a voice,' recalled Watling.

'So did a skunk name of Jard Horner,' said Larry. 'It struck him as funny. He laughed, said 'stay and fry'. But now he's through laughin'.'

'Who were the two women?' demanded Melrose. 'I'm satisfying your curiosity. You might as well satisfy mine.'

'One of 'em was sick — dyin'.' said Larry.

'That would be a whore called Dorrie,' nodded Melrose. 'Always coughing.' He grimaced. 'That disgusting cough.'

'The other was Belle Fassen,' said Larry. 'Dorrie died while you heroes were settin' the town afire. Belle toted her body out of Hanslow's, then came a'runnin' to the jail to set me free, near got burned to death savin' me.'

'Oh, the bawd with the scar,' sneered Melrose. 'What an insult to the eyesight *she* was. My uncle and aunt — being so high-minded — maintained a maudlin sympathy for the Fassen woman. Personally, I avoided looking at her.'

'How'd this trail-bum get onto us?' asked Watling.

'Care to answer that, Lawrence?' prodded Melrose.

'Oh, sure,' Watling suddenly remembered. 'He got the letter Dansley wrote you.'

'But before that,' Melrose challenged Larry. 'How did you begin suspecting . . . ?'

'You did a lousy job of burnin' the fake uniforms,' muttered Larry.

'Ah, yes, so you said,' grinned Melrose. 'Quite the detective, aren't you? All it took was a button and a fragment of material. But now I'm sure you're regretting your snooping expedition. What did it win you after all? Hal, I can keep Dansley's mouth shut by mailing him the two thousand he demanded. But this snooper . . . '

'He goes now,' Watling told him. 'Don't worry. This won't be noisy.'

As he left the connecting doorway to advance on Larry, he transferred his pistol to his other hand and, from inside his left sleeve, produced a thin-bladed knife.

'So-long, Lawrence,' said Melrose.

He reached into a drawer. When his right hand reappeared, it was gripping a .38 Smith & Wesson and the muzzle was aimed at Larry. Two more steps Watling moved toward Larry, after which Larry's back-up decided it was time he announced himself. The taller Texan was suddenly looming in the doorway Watling had vacated, his right hand gunfilled.

'Drop that purty pistol — the sticker too!' he ordered.

What happened during the next minute happened fast, but the veteran trouble-shooters were equal to it, caught up in a life or death situation all too familiar to them — yet another showdown.

Watling made the fatal mistake of whirling and firing. While Stretch threw himself to one side with the Colt roaring, Larry slid from his chair to the floor and reached to his fallen sidearm. He heard the bark of Melrose's pistol and felt a tongue of fire lash at his left shoulder-blade, but got his hand to his holster and emptied it. He rolled and, and he came half-upright, Melrose rose to his feet to aim down at him. His Colt boomed first and, with his starched dress shirt bloody, Melrose shuddered and began sagging. The .38 barked again, the slug boring into expensive carpet. Watling was reeling drunkenly. The nickel-plated pistol discharged, but downward, the bullet further damaging the carpet. Then he sprawled on his back and breathed his last.

'Better get this done muy pronto,' growled Larry, rising.

He moved around behind the desk while Stretch hunkered beside Watling's body. Melrose's wallet — morocco — was so well-filled that Larry deemed it discreet to leave two $100 bills in it. Stretch, just as impressed by the Watling bankroll, emptied it of all save a hundred and a fifty.

The five shots had shocked the

patrons down below, not to mention two officers of the San Francisco PD entering the gaming-room. Gerhane and Kosleck flashed their badges and made for the stairs.

'Tagged the other one up to that other room,' Stretch was explaining, while he and Larry stowed banknotes in their pockets. 'Just watched and waited. Close, huh?'

'You done good,' Larry commended him. 'Real good.' He heard a pounding and bellowing, a demand the door be opened. 'Shootin's all over!' he called. 'And that door ain't locked!'

The detectives barged in to gawk at Watling's body and two uncommonly tall westerners unhurriedly ejecting spent shells and reloading their Colts.

'Hol-eee Mother Murphy!' gasped Gerhane. 'Is Cody's wild west show in town?'

Careful with those six-shooters, you two,' warned Kosleck.

'We're always careful,' frowned Stretch. 'What the hell? Think we don't savvy how to handle our own hoglegs?'

The Texans holstered their weapons, fished out their makings and made ready to be interrogated. Anticipating the first question, Larry drawled, 'The other one, Miller, he's back of the desk and just as dead as Watling.'

Gerhane rushed to the desk, leaned over to peer at the second body, then stared hard at the trouble-shooters and said exactly what they expected him to say.

'You got some explaining to do.'

'Right here?' asked Stretch, lighting his cigarette.

'Right here and *now*,' insisted Gerhane. 'Dave, send for the city coroner's wagon and, while you're about it, tell the swells and the staff the joint's closing.'

After Kosleck hurried out, Gerhane perched on the outer edge of the desk and eyed the tall men challengingly. Larry reseated himself, lit his smoke, invited his partner to get comfortable, then took a risk by reminding the heavy-breathing sergeant, 'You're still pointin' a gun at us, and that ain't polite. Did we blow any holes through that door when you hollered at us?'

'We plumb invited you in,' Stretch said reproachfully.

'Bill Cody's show *must* be in town!' scowled Gerhane. 'And two of his cowboys're a couple of gun-crazy, homicidal lunatics!'

'Second time tonight you've been called crazy, runt,' remarked Stretch. 'That ain't polite neither.'

'Who in blue blazes are you?' demanded Gerhane.

'My partner's Woodville Emerson, called Stretch,' said Larry. 'I'm Lawrence Valentine, called Larry.'

'I'm Sergeant Gerhane, San Francisco police,' growled Gerhane.

'This is friendlier,' approved Stretch. 'Every son gettin' to know who's who.'

'Now, if you've never heard of us, I'd better . . . ' began Larry.

'Wait a minute,' frowned Gerhane,

holstering his pistol. 'Valentine and Emerson? I think maybe I have heard your names.'

'I'd still better set you straight, just so you won't stay so all-fired jumpy,' drawled Larry. 'We ain't law-breakers and no tin star anyplace holds a warrant on us.'

'We're just a couple do-right Texas boys that craves to mind our own blame business, but never get a chance,' Stretch lamented. 'We fight bandidos and killers and all kinds of bad hombres all the time, but not because it pleasures us. Just to stay alive, you know?'

'If you were wanted in this city, I'd know it,' Gerhane acknowledged. 'All right now, we got two stiffs here and two live and heavily-armed buckaroos from what west coast people call the wide open spaces. I see guns on the floor and a knife too, also some bullet-holes, so you're gonna claim you gunned Miller and Watling in self-defence. I'm listening. Start convincing me.'

He glanced to the cigar-box, hesitated a moment, then helped himself to a Havana and lit up.

'It's a long story,' said Larry. 'Before I start tellin' it, how about you read that letter.'

'That'un,' said Stretch, pointing. 'Right there on the desk.'

Gerhane first inspected the envelope.

'It's addressed to Miller,' he noted.

'Big city lawmen're smart,' Larry remarked to Stretch.

'Yup,' agreed Stretch. 'They don't miss nothin'.'

'No smart talk,' cautioned Gerhane. 'Smart talk me, and it's the tank for you.'

'Hell, runt,' protested Stretch. 'Can he do that? Drown us — just because we joshed him?'

'The tank is what we call a holding cell,' Gerhane said impatiently. 'You wouldn't like the company you'd be with — deadbeats, panhandlers, stumblebums, all kinds of street trash.'

'If you're through tryin' to spook us,

read that damn letter,' urged Larry.

Gerhane had read only the first line when he was distracted; Larry had removed his jacket and shirt and Stretch was rolling his undershirt up to his neck.

'Now what the hell're you doing?' he frowned.

'Ought to be some booze here somewhere,' Larry told his partner.

''Scuse us, Sarge,' said Stretch. 'You likely didn't notice. My ol' buddy got creased.'

'I don't see any blood,' argued Gerhane.

'You can't see it from where you're settin',' said Larry.

Gerhane slid from the desk and came closer to stare at the ugly slash across Larry's shoulderblade. He winced as the taller Texan, having found a decanter of high quality bourbon, wet a bandana and began swabbing the gash. Gerhane winced. Larry didn't.

'Just a nick, runt,' offered Stretch. 'It don't bleed no more.'

'Tough guys,' remarked Gerhane.

'Aw, we ain't so tough,' shrugged Stretch. 'It's just, if we get bullet-stung, we try not to get all het up about it.'

'We'd as soon keep our minds on them that's shootin' at us,' explained Larry, 'make sure they don't get time to put one in our heads or our guts, or dead centre. Hey, Gerhane, are you ever gonna read that letter?'

Gerhane perched on the desk again and, while he read Dansley's demand, Larry tucked his undershirt in and re-donned shirt and jacket. When Gerhane raised his eyes again, after reading the letter twice, Stretch had broken out glasses; the trouble-shooters were working on generous shots of bourbon, putting it away as if it were water.

'I'm interested, and that's putting it mild,' he assured them. 'What this Dansley jasper wrote indicates Miller got into something big. Not so long ago, he was a two-bit bunko man, then he suddenly came by big bucks, enough to set himself up in this deluxe gyp-joint. So you're the hot shots who caught onto some big deal the way Dansley says? All right, I want to hear about it.'

So it had to be told again, but a fuller account now. As well as describing the means by which eight desperadoes masquerading as troopers had looted the Dryden cache and reduced a small town to smoldering rubble, the Texans could and did recount the damning admissions made by a couple of rogues who assumed Larry wouldn't live to repeat a word they said. Still discreet, still determined the Drydens be kept in ignorance of their nephew's true character, Larry never once referred to him as Melrose. Also, the almost emptying of two wallets was, they mutually decided, their own business and no concern of the San Francisco PD.

During the telling of it, Kosleck returned with men from the coroner's department; the bodies were removed and Kosleck stayed on to hear Larry's closing remarks.

'Take 'em downtown now, right?' he challenged Gerhane.

'Where else?' sighed Gerhane.

'Just a doggone minute,' growled Stretch. 'You sayin' you're gonna arrest us — you don't believe a damn thing we told you? Hell, it's the stone-cold truth.'

'No charges against you.' Gerhane said reassuringly. 'But your statement has to be on record. I don't know how cowtown sheriffs deal with you independents, but . . . '

'We know all about affidavits and such,' shrugged Larry. 'We've travelled the route.'

'There's something else,' said Gerhane. To Kosleck he remarked. 'Everything I got from these wild boys ties in with what we sweated out of Vormann.'

'Is that so?' frowned Kosleck.

'The Dutchman's gonna weep,' Gerhane predicted with a grin. 'The stuff Miller unloaded on him *was* stolen property, and Valentine and his buddy have named the owner. That bauble's an heirloom, Dave. Lady name of Dryden can probably prove ownership. It was willed to her and, even if her copy was lost when Curran was torched, there'll be a duplicate in some lawyer's files.'

'So Carrie'll get it back?' prodded Larry.

'Her chances're getting better all the time,' said Gerhane. 'Come on, let's get out of here.'

Later, at police headquarters, the Lone Star drifters were duly impressed by the size of the squad-room, uniformed and plainclothes cops moving in and out, everything a'bustle, but doggedly masked their feelings, appearing bored while having their statement recorded by Detective Kosleck, seated by a desk at which he pounded a typewriter.

'Never saw one of these before, have you?' he presumed, half-way through his chore. 'It's called a typewriter.'

'We've seen 'em,' Larry assured him.

'Them telephone contraptions too.'

'And street lights that come on without no hombre touchin' a firestick to 'em,' muttered Stretch. 'And rigs than run along the streets on rails.'

'Not your first time in a big city?' asked Kosleck.

'We've been here before,' said Larry. 'And Chicago, Denver, El Paso, Cheyenne, a lot of big towns.'

'We don't like 'em,' said Stretch. 'No place for the likes of us.'

In his private office, Captain Emmett O'Keefe was remarking to Gerhane, 'They've been here before you know. Old friend of mine used to be on the force, retired now. He still mentions them once in a while. It was a long time ago and, believe me, they triggered many a donnybrook while they were in our fair city.'

'Made the west coast papers too,' said Gerhane. 'That's where I first read of 'em. Well, I'm satisfied they're men of their word. How about you?'

'I'm satisfied too,' declared O'Keefe.

'We were suspicious of Miller, had him pegged for a sharp felon, and they've verified everything. We can close the book on this one, Paddy, so we owe those old cowhands. And I go along with your idea of restoring the necklace to Mrs Dryden. It'll be complicated, but not too much. You can tell Valentine and Emerson we'll start the machinery.'

They discussed that aspect of the affair at some length, after which Gerhane moved out of the squadroom to find Kosleck finishing off and the Texans appending their signatures where indicated. While he outlined the procedure through which the heirloom's rightful owner could recover same, they hung on his every word.

'You got all that, runt?' asked Stretch.

'I got all that,' nodded Larry.

'Next question,' said Gerhane. 'The lady and her husband were just about wiped out, their store burned and their cash stolen by the Miller gang, so can they scratch up enough for railroad fare from New Mexico?'

Stretch's face was suddenly blank. Larry stroked his chin and assumed a pensive expression; he was thinking of the wealth stuffed into their pockets and the contents of the satchel in Phin Madigan's safe.

'Well, uh huh, yeah,' he said. 'I think they'll just about manage it.'

'They can ask for me,' offered Gerhane. 'The — uh — present custodian of the heirloom will surender it, you can count on that. And I hope the lady'll heed my advice. I'm gonna suggest an article so valuable ought to be kept in a safe deposit vault in a San Francisco bank. Tell the Drydens to ask for me soon as they arrive, or wire me they're on their way, and I'll take care of them personally.'

'We appreciate that,' said Larry. 'They'll appreciate it too.'

'Meanwhile, I guess you'll be on the next train back to Santa Fe,' said Gerhane.

'Any idea when . . . ?' began Stretch.

'Be at the depot eight-thirty in the morning,' urged Gerhane. 'Bound to be eastbounds leaving about that time.' As they got to their feet, he grinned wryly and remarked, 'Short stay, huh? But eventful?'

'You could say that,' agreed Larry.

Gerhane and Kosleck farewelled them cordially and, upon being asked, estimated the cab fare from this building to the Madigan Hotel. The tall men thanked them and, a few moments later, were outside and hailing a cab. This cabman proved less larcenous to out-of-towners; they were charged the fare nominated by the detectives.

They slept comfortably this night, rose for an early breakfast, retrieved Larry's saddlebags while being wished a pleasant journey and, toward sundown, aboard an eastbound train and with the prospect of an overnight stop in Hacketsville, had come to a decision.

The Hacketsville undertaker doubled as a stone mason, offering not only dignified funerals but a fine variety of headstones inscribed as requested. A deal was made. The undertaker was willing to place hand on Bible and swear an oath of secrecy when Larry extracted two $100 bills from the satchel and held them under his nose.

'For what you're offering, you get anything you ask for,' he fervently declared.

'It's nothin' you can't take care of, friend,' soothed Larry.

'And quiet,' stressed Stretch. 'Has to be done quiet.'

Larry helped himself to pad and pencil.

'This is what we want on the headstone.'

When he had finished, the undertaker studied what he had printed. 'Todd Melrose, R.I.P.' Also the date of death.

'That'd be Friday of just a couple weeks ago,' he frowned.

'Right,' nodded Larry. 'This hombre flopped on your doorstep, good-lookin' young feller, but hurtin' bad. Told you his name just before he cashed in. You're a charitable man, so you gave him decent burial. That's what you tell a couple name of Dryden if they should ever come here and ask to see the grave. He was their nephew.'

'Is this Melrose really dead?' asked the undertaker.

'What d'you care?' countered Stretch. 'You ain't plantin' a genuine stiff. We're talkin' about a fake grave.'

'He's dead sure enough,' said Larry. 'But it's worth the two hundred for the Drydens to believe he's buried here and that he died just like I've said.'

'Leave it to me.' The undertaker accepted the $200 and gave his word. 'A mound about six feet long, the headstone, I can set it up the way you want. Pleasure doing business with you gents.'

The tallest of the eastbound's passengers had been assigned a two bed room of the Pacifico Hotel. Before retiring, they finally got around to tallying the contents of the satchel, now somewhat bulkier for the addition of the greenbacks taken from their most recent victims. They were taken aback. They had recovered Zack Dryden's $25,000 — plus $1,700.

'Our arithmetic always was lousy,' grouched Larry.

Arriving in Santa Fe, they transferred to a southbound freight. Reaching Davistown, they unloaded and saddled the sorrel and pinto and made straight for the headquarters of Sheriff Owen Heenan, there to learn that the prisoner Rollo Dansley had been buried the day before.

'We noticed he was getting edgy,' Heenan told them. 'Something about a letter he was expecting. No letter came for him, so he must've cracked.'

As the boss-lawman recounted Dansley's escape attempt, Larry conjured up a mental picture of the jailer, Saul Bowker, and his old Navy Colt holstered between navel and crotch. It transpired that, while being escorted to the ablution block, Dansley had seized the weapon. But Bowker, with speed and strength that belied his age, gripped Dansley's wrist during the ensuing struggle, forcing the cocked percussion pistol's muzzle away from himself; Dansley lived only a couple of minutes after it discharged.

Headed for Curran County, the drifters again speculated on the question that had preoccupied them since their departure from San Francisco. How were they faring, the Drydens and Belle Fassen, the only three inhabitants they really cared about?

The morning of their arrival, they at once noted the changes. Beyond the end of the main street was a black mound, all debris and rubble had been piled there. Just beyond the other end, lumber had been unloaded. Rebuilding was under way, the new Sperlman Bank lacking only its roofing, an adobe and timber jail under construction, a clapboard structure on the site of what had been Hanslow's Bar with a freshly-painted sign proclaiming it to be the

Square Deal Saloon and, much to the Texans' approval, another sign outside a building taking shape on its original site, Dryden's Emporium.

A lawman strange to them, his badge gleaming, his eyes alert, watched them dismount in front of the half-completed store and enter. The Drydens greeted them warmly.

'Never doubted you'd keep your promise,' declared Dryden.

'We know poor Todd's dead, know it in our hearts,' murmured Carrie. 'But were you able to find out . . . ?'

'It happened just like you feared.' When it came to white lies, Larry was always convincing. 'That's how them fakers knew where to find your stash, Zack. But they've paid for what they did, all eight of 'em dead now. And Todd did get decent burial.'

'Where?' asked Carrie.

'Town called Hacketsville,' offered Stretch.

'They left him for dead, but he had just strength enough to reach the

Hacketsville undertaker,' said Larry. 'Gave his name just before he died. And that undertaker's a real Christian gentleman. It's what you'd call a decent grave. Hacketsville's a long way from here but, if you ever do visit it . . . '

'We'll try,' sighed Dryden. 'But the loan Karl Sperlman made me accept, we need every dollar of it for rebuilding, laying in stock, getting back into business.'

'Whatever the banker loaned you, you can settle with him,' Larry said encouragingly. The Drydens' eyes widened as he produced a thick wad. 'All there, Zack, the whole twenty-five thousand.'

'But — how . . . ?' began Dryden.

'We had to fight all eight of 'em,' shrugged Larry.

'Not all of 'em at the same time,' said Stretch. 'Two then one, then three, then two more in 'Frisco.'

'We took back what they robbed you of,' declared Larry. 'That's yours, Zack, no question. And we got some more news for you.'

Carrie's eyes shone as he instructed her as to how to recover the heirloom, a journey to San Francisco which should be a pleasure trip, and obliging sergeant of detectives waiting to help them with all formalities. The gratitude of the Drydens brought a lump to Stretch's throat. Dryden gripped their hands. Carrie hugged them.

When they left the Drydens, the sound of a familiar voice raised in song drew them to the new saloon. Belle Fassen, strong-willed Belle, was still doing what she did best and stoically accepting her disfigurement. She flashed them a smile after finishing her song, laid her guitar aside and joined them at the bar, while they sampled whiskey of a quality far exceeding that of the rotgut once served by Bart Hanslow. After greeting them, she reported changes for the better.

'Some townfolk, but mostly Half Circle hands, ran them out of the territory,' she told them. 'You can guess who. Hanslow and his hard case friends, and Billy Ackers and Sam Phipps. We have a new sheriff. He was the blacksmith at Bar Six until Karl Sperlman persuaded him to take over. And this place is run by Chuck Nichols now, a nice man who was weary of being a whiskey drummer and looking for a place to settle. He had some money saved and Sperlman advanced him a little extra, enough to build this new saloon and stock it.'

'A lot of toilin' out there,' mused Larry, glancing to the batwings. 'Curran folks're keepin' busy, so it looks like there'll be a fine new town here.'

'But you won't stay on for all the rebuilding,' she guessed.

'We never stay on, Belle,' said Larry.

'And we scarce ever come back to a place we've been before,' shrugged Stretch. 'Only reason we came back to Curran was to kind of — uh — make them Dryden's some happier'n they've been.'

She studied them knowingly.

'Did it again, didn't you? If Zack and Carrie are happier now, there can be only one reason. You took care of everything, tracked those robbers and recovered every dollar of Zack's nest-egg. And you did it for all of us, not just the Drydens, but the whole town.'

'Well,' said Larry. 'We didn't like what they did to Curran, to you and Dorrie — and us.'

'But now you'll ride away and forget it — right?' she challenged.

'It's over, Belle,' said Larry. 'And we got no reason to linger.'

'Our feet itch again,' explained Stretch.

'Take care?' she begged. 'Remember what I said before? People need you, people you haven't met yet.'

Other locals were wandering in with a thirst. She talked with them a while longer, then returned to where she had left her guitar and began another song. It was then that they left, moving out into the sunlight to untether their horses and swing astride.

On their way out of Curran, they paused to watch workmen rebuilding the jail. Grim memories bedeviled them as they rolled and lit cigarettes.

'Close,' Stretch remarked. 'We near got par-boiled in there. Would've been a helluva way to go, huh?'

'It wasn't our time to die,' muttered Larry. 'Somethin' prodded Belle and she came a'runnin'.'

'Close,' Stretch repeated.

'What the hell?' shrugged Larry. 'Not our first close call, nor our last.'

'That's great, just Jim-dandy,' grouched Stretch. 'You thinkin', wherever we go from here, we'll ride into another ruckus?'

'Don't we always?' challenged Larry.

'Yup, we always do,' nodded Stretch, as they rode on. 'And I still don't savvy why. I mean, a couple peaceable, harmless hombres like us. Why does it always have to happen?'

'Don't ask me why,' Larry said irritably. 'What can I tell you? It's our hex, and things ain't gonna get any better for us — and that's the way it's always been.'

'Ain't that the truth,' Stretch agreed.

He shrugged fatalistically and they travelled away from Curran, headed nowhere in particular.

THE END

THE DUDE MUST DIE
WAIT FOR THE JUDGE
HOLD 'EM BACK!
WELLS FARGO DECOYS
WE RIDE FOR CIRCLE 6
THE CANNON MOUND GANG
5 BULLETS FOR JUDGE BLAKE
BEQUEST TO A TEXAN
THEY'LL HANG BILLY FOR SURE
SLOW WOLF AND DAN FOX
THE NO NAME GANG
DOUBLE SHUFFLE
CHALLENGE THE LEGEND